TORRAN

A CRASHLAND COLONY ROMANCE

LESLIE CHASE

TORRAN

Editing by Sennah Tate

Copyright 2019 Leslie Chase
All rights reserved

This is a work of fiction intended for mature audiences. All names, characters, businesses, places, events and incidents are products of the author's imagination. Any resemblance to actual persons, living or dead, or actual events is purely coincidental.

❦ Created with Vellum

*Dedicated to all my writing buddies. As always the Saucy
Sprints writing group helped me get this book written, and
the Tuesday Terrors kept me focused when I needed it.
Thank you all!*

1

LISA

I woke to darkness in a space the size of a coffin. The brochures warned us about hibernation sickness, but I hadn't expected it to be this bad. My head felt like a mule had kicked it, my joints burned, and when I pried open my eyes I *couldn't see.*

A moment of panic later, I realized the stasis tube's lights hadn't come on. The only illumination was a faint glimmer shining through the cracks around the edge of the tube's door. A door that should have sprung open automatically.

Great, so what else has gone wrong? I took a deep breath and tried to calm down. I was alive, and I'd made it. The *Wandering Star* must have reached Arcadia Colony — otherwise it wouldn't have woken me up.

A smile spread across my face despite the pain. Another world! Escape from Earth and all its troubles, the water wars and the pollution. So what if some systems failed on arrival? I'd made it to my new home.

Bracing myself against the wall, I pushed the door as hard as I could. It took all my strength to move it, but it did move. Bright light poured in through the gap making me wince and squeeze my eyes shut. I threw my weight against the door, pushing it wide and tumbling out onto the cold metal floor of the colony pod.

Everything seemed to be at an odd angle, the light was far too bright, and an unsettling hum filled the air. For a moment I let myself worry — had something gone wrong? Had the pod malfunctioned, woken me in the depths of space with months to go before we arrived? But fresh air filled the room with the scent of alien plants, reassuring me. A sweet and pungent smell like nothing on Earth filled my nostrils and I laughed aloud, lying back to let myself adjust to the new atmosphere.

"Sis, is that you? I'm stuck." Malcolm's petulant voice pulled me back to myself and I sat up with a groan. *Great, little brother, you're not even going to let me enjoy the first minute of a new planet before you start complaining.*

Unfair, of course. If he'd gotten out of his stasis tube first, I'd have been demanding he let me out right away. Still, I'd have liked just a few minutes to soak in the wonder of the new world.

"Coming, Mal," I grumbled, pushing myself off the cold floor with an effort and looking around. The two coffin-sized hibernation tubes took up most of the space in the small room, with lockers for our personal possessions filling the rest. Bright sunlight streamed in through the transparent roof, and that was the only light. I frowned — when we'd boarded the pod there'd been dozens of holographic displays to look at, but all were dead now. This wasn't how I'd expected to wake up.

As I struggled to pry open my brother's tube, I heard other colonists moving around outside. The pod held three families, all winners of the colony lottery system back on Earth, and from the sound of it we weren't the only ones having trouble.

First things first, let's get Malcolm out, I told myself, and with a final heave managed to pull the doors of his tube wide. Malcolm grinned up at me and threw his arms round my neck.

"We made it!" He shouted the words, petulance forgotten as soon as he was free. "We really did, didn't we?"

I grinned, lifting him out of the tube. It wasn't as easy as it used to be, my little brother was growing fast, but I managed to get him on his feet. We were both a little unsteady, staggering to our lockers and pulling out our wristbands. They ought to link up to the colony computer network, but the red 'no signal' light came on instead. Not even local wifi from the colony pod. That wasn't right.

"Maybe the others know what's going on?" Malcolm asked hopefully, switching his off and on again. No change. "There's probably a power outage or something."

I didn't think that sounded right. Back on Earth power outages had been a common problem, but out here on a new world with brand new infrastructure things ought to be better. The wristbands only had short range radio links but surely they should pick up *something?*

Standing around looking at the error message wouldn't tell us anything, so we made our way into the communal space outside. The big round room was meant for all the colonists to share, a dining room and meeting room in one. The doors to the other colonist families' rooms were still shut — we were the first to emerge, though I heard our neighbors' voices. It didn't sound like anyone was in any trouble, so I decided to leave them alone.

"Is it just me, or are we on a slope?" Malcolm asked as we walked to the long table and sat down. I frowned, wanting to say it was just the hibernation sickness. But he was right. The room tilted to the side, only a little but enough to notice. I remembered the briefings — the pod ought to have picked a nice flat safe place to land.

"You rest here, I'll see what's going on," I told my brother, pushing myself back to my feet with an effort and making my way forward. If none of the others were ready to go yet that suited me fine. It gave me the chance to be the first of our party to set foot on Arcadia.

To be on the safe side, I stopped in our secure store and picked up a rifle. The wildlife wasn't supposed to be very dangerous, but then the Arcadia Colony Company had packed the laser rifles for a reason and I'd feel better with one slung on my back.

Most of the pod was storage, with our living quarters at the core. The secure store and the sickbay were next. Beyond that I had the choice of the engineering bay or the cargo holds. Without power, engineering's external ramp would be hell to get open, so the cargo hold it was.

As soon as I opened the hatch, I saw that something had gone badly wrong. The stored equipment, everything we should need to set up our new home on a fresh world, had been secured to the walls.

Now it lay scattered across the floor, the cabling that ought to hold it in place torn loose from the fittings. I blinked at the devastation. Had we *crashed?*

"Doesn't matter," I said aloud, trying to convince myself. "We made it down in one piece, and someone will come and help us if we need it. We made it to Arcadia and everything's going to be fine."

Trying to believe that, I made my way through the devastation to the outer door. I wasn't about to let a lack of power stop me from seeing my new home, so I pried open a panel to reach the emergency crank.

Warm air gusted inside as the door slowly slid open, carrying that strong sweet scent. The light was bright and somehow different, looking subtly wrong to my Earth-raised eyes. I shaded my eyes, feeling nauseous but unwilling to let that stop me.

Yeah, we'd come down in the wrong place. That

much was obvious at a glance — trees stood all around us. I'd seen pictures of the land we'd won in the colony lottery, good grassy plains beside a lake.

This was a forest on a hillside. I hoped we hadn't missed by much because I doubted the colony pod would take off again any time soon.

Our location wasn't all that was wrong. Probably every colonist had the same obsessive interest in our new home I did, and we'd all been through every bit of data we could find. I'd walked through Arcadia's forests in a dozen virtual tours and not one of them showed these strange purple trees. Frowning, I tried to shake off the feeling of wrongness and jumped down from the ramp.

My boots sank into alien soil and everything else left my mind. *I'm standing on an alien planet*, I thought exultantly. My heart pounded and my mouth was dry as I sank into a crouch, digging my fingers into the dirt.

Free of Earth, free and safe to make a new life for myself and for Malcolm. We'd made it out of the grinding poverty and now everything would be alright. A huge grin spread across my face.

If only our parents could be here with us, it would have been perfect.

Refusing to let that thought darken my mood, I turned to look at the colony pod. Back on Earth it had been shiny and new, pristine at the start of our journey. We'd only seen it once when we boarded and got into our stasis tubes for the long trip, but I remembered that as though it was yesterday.

For me, it *was* yesterday — I'd spent the months of flight frozen in stasis.

The pod hadn't been so lucky. Its surface streaked with soot and bare spaces where insulation tiles had torn away, it had clearly been through a rough landing. I swallowed, thanking my lucky stars we'd come through it intact.

"What happened?" I asked aloud, taking a few steps back to get a better look at the damaged pod. "You were meant to come down nice and smooth on good farmland. What went wrong?"

The pod stayed silent, keeping its secrets, and I started to circle it. Best to survey the damage before wandering off into the forest, though I wanted more than anything to see my new homeworld.

My wristband beeped as I made my way around the ship, catching me by surprise. I grinned in relief, answering it and hoping that it was a call from the colony authorities with an explanation. No luck: it was just Malcolm calling from inside the pod.

"You'd better get back in here, sis," he told me. "The Carringtons are up and about, and they want a meeting."

Of course they did. All through our short training the Carringtons had assumed that they were in charge, and that got old fast. If there was one thing about the colony lottery I didn't like, it was being teamed up with that family at random.

They weren't wrong, though. We did need to get together and sort out what had happened.

"I'll be there in a minute," I told Malcolm, signing off before he could protest. Mr. Carrington might want me to hurry back, but I didn't owe him anything.

I checked the wristband again. Local signals showed, but still nothing further afield. Nothing from any of the other colony pods, or the *Wandering Star*, or the satellites that should be in orbit.

Even if it couldn't put me in touch with anyone else though, I didn't have to be alone out here. The virtual companion program had sounded like a silly idea back on Earth but in the spooky silence of this alien forest I had more appreciation for it.

A couple of flicked switches and Henry appeared beside me with a bark. The faintly translucent Pomeranian holo-puppy bounded around my feet and I couldn't help grinning.

I'd never had a pet back on Earth, not even a simulated one. Having Henry jumping around like a mad thing took the edge off the eerie quiet and I felt a little better as I continued my circuit of the pod.

We'd definitely crashed, and we were lucky it hadn't come down any harder. Maybe, with a lot of work, our pod might fly again. I didn't want to trust it, though, not with the engines banged up like they were. At least the pod's autopilot had found a relatively open area in the woods to come down, but even so we'd smashed into a few trees as we landed.

Could be worse. We could have started a forest fire. It looked like there'd been a lot of rain recently and if our landing rockets had started any fires, they'd burned out fast. I tried to take comfort from that, but the feeling of wrongness nagged at me. The trees looked nothing like the Arcadian trees we'd seen in the simulators and there was no sign of the planet-wide communication network that the Arcadia Colony Company had promised us.

"Don't be silly, Lisa," I told myself, hoping that speaking aloud would help me convince myself. "This has to be Arcadia. Anything else is impossible. Right?"

Henry turned and looked up at me, barking reassurances. They felt as hollow as my words. But he did give me an idea. I crouched next to the holo-puppy and pointed to a flower, a bright red point amongst the purple trees.

"What's that, Henry?" I asked. Our companion holograms were loaded with data on Arcadian plants and animals — he ought to be able to tell me all about them.

Instead he whined and nuzzled at my leg, his built-in forcefield letting me feel the touch. It was like being nuzzled by a ghost.

My frown deepened and I turned to another plant, a weird fractal fern. "How about that?"

Nothing but a whine from Henry. I tried again with one of the purple-leaved trees. Nope. None of the plants were in Henry's database.

I couldn't avoid the obvious conclusion any longer. An empty pit opened up in my stomach as I admitted what I'd known deep down since I stepped out of the pod. Somehow we'd ended up on the wrong planet.

By the time I returned to the pod, everyone had gathered in the central room. Mr. Carrington (never Simon, he'd made that quite clear on our first meeting) paced around the circular room, his three sons watching quietly from their seats at the wall. The whole family had been distant through training and I hardly knew them.

Alex and Maria Dietrich had pried open an inspection hatch and the two of them worked together, their daughter Tania handing them tools. She was about Malcolm's age, and I hoped that they'd be friends. There wasn't much hope with the Carrington boys — back on Earth they'd made it clear that they were adults now and had no time for hanging around with children.

Everyone looked around as I came in, and I waited until I had their attention. Now that they were all staring at me it seemed silly, but I had to tell them what I'd learned. *Better just say it*, I thought.

"I don't think this is Arcadia," I said.

"That's not possible," Mr. Carrington interrupted before I could say more. He was the oldest of our little group, leading his sons out of the remains of Britain with a fierce discipline that was a little off-putting. "No time for foolish jokes, Lisa. We need to get in touch with the *Wandering Star* and find out why we're in the wrong place."

"We do," I agreed, trying not to let him get to me.

"But we're not just in the wrong place, we're on the *wrong planet*."

"Impossible," he said again, face reddening as I contradicted him. "I know that this is exciting but don't let it go to your head, young lady."

I bristled at his tone. "None of the plants are in the database, and the sunlight is the wrong color."

He shook his head briskly. "We'll see about that. Ms. Dietrich will get the power working and then we'll contact the other colonists, find out what's what. Until then, we'd best do some scouting. I'll take my boys out and get a feel for the lay of the land. Why don't you pack us some lunch, Lisa? We'll be gone for a few hours at least."

My jaw tightened, and I was about to say something I'd regret when Maria Dietrich caught my eye and shook her head. There was a spark of amusement in her eyes that made it easier to put aside my annoyance.

"Do not be silly, Mr. Carrington," she said, her faint German accent coloring her words. "What will you see that Lisa hasn't? We do not wish to risk losing you or your sons. Wherever we have landed, there will be unknown dangers and we need you to protect us."

Carrington's face reddened, but he nodded. The suggestion that his family would be the protectors of our little colony seemed to mollify him. "Very well, very well. We will stay and protect our new home. David, fetch out the rifles."

His oldest son nodded quickly and almost ran to open the armory. Both of his brothers practically vibrated with excitement as they waited for him to return. I winced. The Carrington boys seemed to be looking forward to shooting something, and while I didn't mind hunting for our dinner, their cheerful enthusiasm for killing was unpleasant.

But Carrington was right, we might need defenses. Who knew what dangers lurked out there on this unknown planet?

2

TORRAN

The planet rose to strike me like a giant fist and I struggled for control of my ship. Nothing worked, not the thrusters, not the communicator, not the weapons. All around me ships of the Silver Band rained from the sky, drained of power and helpless.

Some struck mountains and exploded in balls of fire. Others plowed into the ground, tumbling end over end and disintegrating. I fought to keep the fighter's nose up, to shed as much speed as possible before the inevitable crash.

As much as I would like to claim that my skill brought me down safely, luck had at least as much to do with it. Luck and perhaps fate. Maybe the ancestors still had plans for me.

I came to a stop at last, the ship dead around me. Whatever taveshi weapon drained my power supply had done a thorough job; even the emergency batteries were empty, used up in keeping me safe from the impact. Relatively safe, anyway. I felt like a giant bruise.

"Sundered Space," I swore to myself as I kicked out the window. The cockpit's hatch faced down now, into the planet's surface. "Whose bright idea was it to invade the Tavesh Empire?"

No one answered. I was alone in my ship, and for all I knew alone on this planet. Others must have survived, I told myself. The Silver Band couldn't be reduced to just me.

I didn't need anyone else to answer my question. Zaren, Alpha-Captain and war-leader, led us here to capture the fleeing human colony ship. A foolish, doomed plan that looked to have cost us everything. Cursing again, I called the ancestors' wrath on him and the other Alpha-Captains who'd followed him into this mess.

I'm hardly blameless, I reminded myself as I looked around my new home and caught my breath. *I could have refused the order, challenged my Alpha.*

But Alpha-Captain Terasi had always led us well, and everything happened so fast. I grimaced. If Terasi lived, I would take it up with her when we next met. If not, then the gods had rendered their judgement already. Either way, it didn't help me now.

Our clan made up the scouts of the Silver Band, and that ought to mean I was in my element on a new world. Terasi had led us to find resources and supplies, to find routes to our enemies, to explore… this was just one more planet.

Except that I lacked any of the tools I'd usually use, and I was alone with no pack to help me. I knew nothing of this planet other than that it was off-limits, forbidden to all by the Tavesh Empire.

It could have been worse, I decided. At least the planet seemed pleasant enough. The light of the sun was bright, white, clean. The air smelled fresh in a way that the recycled air I was used to never did, and the flowering plants nearby were beautiful. We could have crashed on a barren world instead.

I picked up a stone, threw it from hand to hand, judging. Gravity felt perhaps a little lower than standard, but not enough to matter. Taking and holding a deep breath let me judge the atmosphere: nothing to fear there. Slightly more oxygen than I was used to, otherwise standard. Watching the shadow of my ship move, I judged that the planet spun quickly, meaning day and night would be short.

I'd been to far worse places and survived.

As pleasant as it was though, I couldn't count on being able to find food. A quick check of my gear gave me the bad news I'd expected — nothing technological worked. The batteries on my blaster pistol and communicator were empty: the taveshi hadn't only targeted the ship's power supply.

I had ration bars, and I had my knives. That was all.

The ancestors did fine with less, I told myself as I looked around for any sign of other survivors. Whatever happened next, I would need a pack around me.

"Here!" I shouted, then howled, hoping the wind

would carry an answer back to me. "Silver Band! I am here!"

The noise might draw a predator. Let it. I could do with a fight, a challenge, something to take my growing frustration out on. But all was quiet.

My fighter steamed as it cooled from the heat of reentry, strange plinking noises coming from it. I looked back, frowning. The landing had torn off a wing and left the nose buried in the muddy soil. Even if I found a way to power her up again, the ship would need a lot of work to get into the air. Let alone back to space.

"Sorry, old friend," I said, raising a hand in blessing at the old fighter I'd been through so much with. "I'll be back for you if I can, but there's no point in me staying here."

Then I turned my back and started walking, picking a direction at random. There was no way of telling where I'd find help, so I might as well trust fate.

Before long I found a stream and started to follow it. Any other survivors would need water, so that seemed as good a way to find them as I could hope for. Around me the wilderness came to life slowly, strange animal noises surrounding me as I walked.

I kept a wary hand on my knife. The trouble with walking along a watercourse was that predators would hunt here too, and I didn't want to be mistaken for something delicious. Nothing leaped out of the long grasses to eat me as I made my way down the stream though.

Ahead, trees rose in a thick forest and I thought I saw smoke. That might be a good sign and I called out again, hoping to find company. I'd need to sleep eventually and without either good shelter or someone to share the watch with, night would be a dangerous time.

No one answered my call. Maybe the smoke wasn't from a crash, or perhaps no one had survived this time. I couldn't tell and I didn't want to guess. But with the sun starting to dip towards the horizon, it was time to look for somewhere safe to sleep. And that meant getting away from the stream and the predators that might follow it.

A rocky outcropping looked like it might at least give me a good vantage point. I made my way up towards it, but as I went, I heard something moving through the long grass off to my right. Careful, prowling, hunting movement. My hand tightened on my knife hilt but I gave no other sign, walking steadily and waiting for whatever was creeping up on me to make its move.

I nearly made it to the rocks before the attack came. The only hint was a sudden rustle in the grass — just enough warning for me to duck aside, spinning and drawing my blade.

Another prytheen warrior sailed through the space I'd just left, hands grasping at thin air, and instinct took me in to counter attack. I jumped onto his back, forcing him down into the soft ground, my blade stabbing at his side. A killing blow if I hadn't stopped at the last moment.

He froze under me and then started to shake with laughter. "Nearly got you that time, Torran," he said, voice muffled by the dirt.

"You idiot, Arvid," I hissed. "I almost killed you."

To make the point, I jabbed him in the side. Not hard enough to break the skin but enough that he couldn't miss the threat. Arvid only laughed harder.

"How many times am I going to have the chance to hunt a scout?" he asked. "Come on, I wasn't about to pass this up."

I growled and stood up, sheathing my knife and shaking my head as he got to his feet. Arvid wasn't exactly a friend, but we'd shared victories and defeats, we'd drunk together, we'd laughed together.

"I'm glad you survived the crash," I said eventually. "And glad I didn't gut you by accident."

"If you ever kill me, it'll be on purpose," he said, brushing himself off and laughing again. "You're too good with a knife to do it accidentally. Sundered Space, Torran, I'm glad you made it down alive. We thought we were going to starve down here, but with a scout? We'll eat like kings."

I snorted at that, unable to quite hide my amusement. Arvid knew as well as I did how hard it would be to test any food we found — I had more experience, but it wasn't magic.

"Wait, 'we'? How many are down here?" I asked, looking around. No sign of any other warriors.

"Two more, waiting at the raider for me to come back with water and any food I can find. Dessus is injured and Tarva is looking after him, plus someone's got to get a fire started."

I didn't recognize the names but I breathed a little easier. Having allies I could rely on would make everything a little easier, and perhaps together we'd be able to get off this blasted planet.

A slim hope, but a lot better than no hope at all. I waited while Arvid gathered the water bottles he'd left by the stream, and then followed him uphill into the trees. The crashed raider wasn't far, and I smelled it before I saw it. Smoke, blood, and spilled oil all mixed into a terrible stench. We couldn't stay here long.

"Look what I found skulking around the water," Arvid cried as he led me into what could generously be called a camp. "This is Torran, one of Terasi's scouts."

"That's us saved then," a grumpy voice answered. The speaker was a short female, face scarred from battle and suspicious. "A scout? Couldn't you have brought back an engineer to fix the damned raider?"

She forced a laugh to show that was a joke. One glance at the ship told me that would be futile. No one would repair that without a space dock, not even Coran's fabled engineers. My fighter had come down hard, but this raider looked like it had hit every tree it could find on the way down.

"My name is Tarva," she said, raising a hand in

greeting. "Dessus is sleeping, the lucky shit. I had to use most of our sleep gel to put him out, it'll be awhile before he wakes up."

I nodded. A prytheen warrior's healing trance would heal most injuries but if the pain was enough to keep him awake Dessus wouldn't be able to take advantage of it.

"What else have you salvaged?" I asked, looking at the makeshift camp and trying to hide my disappointment. This wreck wouldn't help me much.

But at least now I had company. Even if it just meant having someone to keep watch while I slept, it was a big improvement on trying to survive alone.

"Not much survived the crash," Tarva admitted. "A few ration bars, two days' worth perhaps. A medkit, mostly used up on Dessus. Two water flasks. What do you have?"

I sighed and shrugged. "Didn't do any better. A tenday's worth of ration bars and a water decontamination kit, that's all."

Arvid and Tarva exchanged glances. I didn't blame them for being disappointed — we'd all hoped finding other survivors would save us, but it looked like we'd have to save ourselves.

Fortunately, we're warriors of the Silver Band, I told myself. *We can rise to any challenge.*

I hoped that wasn't empty bluster on my part. I looked around the crash site again, catalogued the remains. The burned-out husk of the raider provided shelter, and the water wasn't too far, but that was all that could be said for this as a camp.

Better not to get too attached to it.

"We can't stay here," I told the others. "Maybe we could hunt enough food to survive, but we're low on all other supplies and I don't intend to live the life of a hunter-gatherer. There will be other survivors, if we're lucky, ones with better equipment than we have. Even if not, there's strength in numbers."

"How do you expect us to find them?" Tarva growled the question. "Just wander around until we run into an Alpha-Captain and their pack?"

Arvid laughed. "He's a *scout*, Tarva. He knows how to find people on a planet, even if we don't. And it beats staying here, waiting for someone else to come find us."

I smiled and sipped my water quietly. Arvid's faith in my abilities was touching, even if it was misplaced. True, I knew how to survive on a planet better than most warriors of the Silver Band, but even we scouts were used to some technology. Navigating without an inertial map, a communications link, a scanner… this would be a challenge.

One I intended to rise to.

"I cannot promise I will find anyone else," I told the trio. "What I can promise is a better chance than staying here. We will seek other survivors, human or prytheen, and with numbers we will be better able to survive."

Arvid nodded. "I don't plan on sitting on my ass and waiting for rescue. We are warriors of the Silver Band!

Come on, Tarva, do you want that to be the story you sing to your kits? That when the Band got stranded on an alien world you waited for others to conquer it?"

Tarva laughed. "Sure, easy for you to say. You won't have to carry Dessus."

Their bickering had the tone of old friendship and shared hardships, and I envied them that companionship. I'd never had anyone that close, no one I could share triumphs and defeats with.

Perhaps I'll meet someone on this journey, I told myself. It wasn't likely, but why not hope?

"We're agreed then," Arvid said, rapping a dagger on the makeshift table. "As soon as Dessus is ready to travel, we leave and seek out other survivors."

3

LISA

The first days on this new planet were the hardest, but they were also rewarding. Maria and Tania worked on getting the communications systems working and the rest of us focused on survival. The galley matter converter turned any organic matter into a nutrient paste that tasted awful but would keep us alive until the crops grew, but we were grateful for the meat that Carrington and his sons brought in.

Alex Dietrich cleared some of the trees around the colony pod, giving us enough space to test the soil for a farm. That was work I could do, following the instructions with Henry's help. The autodoc in sickbay ran the analysis and I ended up spending a lot of time working there.

The readings were strange, hard to interpret, but at last I concluded that some of our crops would grow here. They'd been engineered to grow damned near anywhere, after all.

It kept me out of Carrington's way, which helped. Despite his promise to stay close and keep us safe, he kept pushing out into the wilderness a little further each day. Unfortunately, every time he killed a new animal he needed to get it tested to see if it was edible. That brought him right back to sickbay and to me.

"You know, you could test them yourself," I said the third time he brought me something new. This time it was about the size of a large rabbit, but that was all that looked familiar about it. The animal had vibrant purple quills instead of fur, and a bright pink frill around its neck. I couldn't help wondering what it would look like without the hole Carrington's laser had burned through it. I picked it up gingerly and lay it on the scanner bed.

"Got to give you something to do, girl," he said, a faint edge in his voice. "Us men are out hunting all day, you ought to make yourself useful somehow."

"I'm testing the soil and—" I stopped at the look on his face. Apparently that didn't count as real work to him, and there was no point in arguing. There never was.

Henry barked at me, saving me from needing to say more. I looked at the display projected above his fluffy holographic head and sighed. "Sure, we can eat most of this if you can catch any more. But not the frill, okay? That's... the computer doesn't know what this stuff is, but it isn't good."

Carrington wrinkled his nose, checking with his own virtual companion. Most colonists picked from the menu of cute animals for our companions, but not him — his took the form of a man in a business suit. In that, as in everything else, Carrington had no imagination or sense of joy.

I tried not to let him bother me too much. That wasn't easy when he insisted on giving me work and then doubted my results. Every time he double checked, and although we'd only found alien life unknown on Earth or Arcadia, he *still* didn't believe that we were on the wrong planet.

Even when his companion confirmed my results Carrington frowned. Without a word he turned to go, and I looked at the quill-rabbit with distaste. Down to me to figure out how to prepare it, apparently.

Our communicators chimed at the same moment, the piercing sound of a high-priority message. Carrington grabbed his rifle as I answered.

"Come quickly," Alex said. "The main hall. Maria has a signal."

Neither of us needed to hear more. For once, we reacted the same, sprinting out of the room, the quill-rabbit lying forgotten on the table behind us. We skidded into the hall, others rushing to join us as Maria gestured for quiet.

"We can't transmit, only listen," she whispered. "But there's a lot to hear."

If anything, that was an understatement. Static hissed and popped as she sorted out the transmissions, some in English, some in an unintelligible alien language. A few were in Galtrade, the alien merchant language that every colonist took a basic course in. I struggled to make out words and didn't like the ones I heard. Attack. Crash. Stranded.

At last Maria tuned us into a signal clear enough to make out, one that identified itself as being from the *Wandering Star*. And what it had to say was a shock to us all. A recorded summary of what had brought us to this planet followed.

The transmission repeated itself and we listened to it over and over before Maria finally muted it.

"So we're not on Arcadia, confirmed," she summarized. "Lisa was right the first time. They are calling this planet Crashland, which seems appropriate enough."

Crashland. I wasn't sure about naming our new home after the disaster that had brought us here, but at least we had a name for it now. More important was why the *Wandering Star* had crashed here.

We'd been attacked by aliens. Fled into space claimed by the isolationist Tavesh Empire. And then we'd crashed along with our attackers. It took listening to the recording a few times to piece it all together, and we still didn't have a full picture of what had happened, but that much was clear. Our alien attackers, the prytheen, were loose on the planet with us and they'd already tried to take over once.

And while the prytheen at the *Wandering Star* were willing to share authority with the ship's captain, we were too far away for that authority to protect us. As near as Maria could work out from the signals, we were half a world away from the ship. The crash had scattered colony pods across the entire planet.

"We must be alert," Mr. Carrington said, clutching his rifle grimly. Did I see a glint of satisfaction in his eyes, or was that just me thinking the worst of him? I couldn't tell. Maybe he was genuinely concerned for our safety, maybe he just liked giving orders, maybe a bit of both. "From now on, no one is to leave the pod without an armed escort."

"Shouldn't we get on our way to the *Wandering Star*, father?" David asked. The eldest of the Carrington boys at twenty-one, he still deferred to his father in every decision. Mr. Carrington shook his head.

"Too far, my boy. Too far to march when we have these ladies to protect."

I bristled at that, drawing breath to speak, but Malcolm got there first.

"Hey," he said, nearly shouting. "My sister doesn't need your protection. Who put you in charge, anyway?"

"In the absence of the Colony Coordinator, someone has to take the lead," Mr. Carrington said smugly, drawing himself up to his full height and looking down his nose at my brother. "Since I have the most experience, I will take on that duty."

His three sons gathered behind him and I knew that there wasn't any winning this fight. If we pushed it things would get ugly fast. All three of Carrington's sons were older than Malcolm and Tania: an election would hang on who got to vote rather than who was the best candidate.

I put my hand on Malcolm's shoulder, trying to make the best of a bad situation. "Fine. Someone has to be in charge, and it might as well be you. We ought to set up some defenses, though."

"Indeed," he said, smiling down at me as though I had finally shown a sign of intelligence. I bit down on an angry retort, letting him speak. "Though there is much else to do. We will be safe enough here if we don't draw attention, and I'll keep an eye out for trouble. I'm an experienced hunter, no one's going to sneak up on me."

Idiot, you can't keep watch the whole time. I let it pass though. No point in picking a fight.

"What's your plan?" Maria asked.

"Clear more of the trees, set up a farm here," Carrington said, a distant look in his eyes. "We're in this for the long term after all. And the men will be busy hunting while you ladies set up the farms."

"If we're going to be setting up permanently, Lisa is right," Alex Dietrich spoke up finally. "We must set up our defenses. If not against the aliens, then against predators. The ultrasonic fences should protect us if we use the updated settings from the *Wandering Star*."

I shuddered, glad we hadn't tried to set up the fence before we'd gotten that message. According to the broadcast, the original settings were worse than useless. Ultrasound intended to keep Arcadian animals at bay would drive the Crashland wildlife into a frenzy instead.

"Very well, set them up if you wish," Carrington replied, sounding annoyed. "For now, get some trees down and I'll get on with bringing in food. We'll need it while the rest of you set up the farms."

Not bothering to listen to any objections, he turned and left, his boys following. I ground my teeth.

"This is stupid," Malcolm muttered. "Why won't he take it seriously? There are aliens out there!"

As his wife turned back to the patched-up communicator, Alex sighed and shook his head. "To be fair, he's probably right. We're out of the way, far from the *Wandering Star*. There's no reason to think the aliens will ever find us here."

"It is a gamble," Maria said. "But it is one he is likely to win. We just have to pray he is right and keep our rifles at hand."

"Then why make a fuss about always going armed and not going far?" Malcolm asked. Maria chuckled sadly.

"Because that puts him in charge. As long as there's a threat, he uses it to keep us in line. And as long as the threat doesn't manifest, he doesn't have to do anything about it."

I swallowed nervously, not liking the sound of that. But it fit. "Can you fix the transmitter? Or maybe reach someone closer?"

Contact with the other colonists might help — especially if a larger pod had come down nearby. Just having the option of somewhere to go would make me feel a lot better. But Maria shook her head. "I can fix the damage, ja. Unfortunately the transmitter is in a poor position here, and unless we reposition it we will not get a signal far. If there were satellites in orbit, then certainly. Without them, there is nothing I can do. No one will hear us."

"Great." I stuck my hands in my pockets and looked around the room. "I guess we'd better get to work clearing trees."

The next few days passed peacefully enough, though the Carringtons were ever more annoying in their assumed authority. It wasn't enough that Mr. Carrington bossed us around, his sons copied his attitude easily and thoughtlessly.

To be fair, the four of them brought in enough food for us all, though they never stopped reminding us where our meals came from. Quill-rabbit turned out to be good eating, and the ship's nutrient paste (while disgusting) added the vitamins we needed to our diet. Maria kept working the radio, pulling in updates and mapping the settlements she could detect.

One night over dinner Maria dropped another bombshell. "There is a settlement nearby. One of the big colony pods came down in the mountains to the south. Close enough to reach perhaps."

Carrington sniffed. "Perhaps over known terrain. Through these woods? It would be a long walk, and a dangerous one. No, better we stay here."

"We can take the rover," Malcolm said excitedly, and

Tania nodded quickly. I grinned. Malcolm had *loved* driving the hover vehicle during training back on Earth, and here was a chance to put it to use. Carrington gave the two children a withering look, though.

"Hardly safe," he said. "We don't even know that there is a path to the mountains large enough for the rover. First we must make ourselves secure here. Then, perhaps, we can spare someone to try the journey and say hello to our neighbors."

Maria and I exchanged glances. We knew better. Carrington didn't intend to give up his authority here until he had to. There didn't seem much point in saying that out loud, though.

"Perhaps we should make contact now, just in case," I suggested, trying to sound meek and hoping that he'd listen. "In an emergency it might be good to have access to somewhere with a better medical facility."

Carrington's smile was as fake as a plastic flower. "Nonsense, Lisa, you should have more confidence in yourself. You can manage anything we need with our sickbay and autodoc."

"But what if Lisa gets sick?" Malcolm asked. Carrington's face pinched, the smile vanishing.

"Then we'll face that problem when it turns up," he snapped. "We can't risk the journey. Not with only one rover, and the warning that there are dangerous animals out there. Too much to lose, and too much else that we have to work on."

The rest of us exchanged glances. He wasn't wrong,

exactly. The rover was a tough little vehicle, able to hover over most obstacles, but pushing through forested hills without guidance still sounded like a good way to drop it down a crevice or something.

On the other hand, it conveniently kept us here in his power. Not something any of us were comfortable with, but what could we do? Even assembling the rover would take at least a day and there was a lot of other work we needed to get on with.

"Fine," I said after a while. "But once the farm's set up, we have to take a trip out and establish contact. Eventually we'll need more medicines if nothing else."

The autodoc wasn't designed to run for long on its own. Even just testing the soil and the animals had run down some of its supplies and Carrington knew it. Reluctantly, he nodded.

"We'll revisit the question then," he agreed, fake smile back. "And we'll scout the terrain in that direction while we work."

That was the best we would get, I thought. A few weeks or months of this didn't seem too bad and once there was a route to another settlement I wouldn't feel so trapped.

WE ALL TOOK turns taking samples of everything we could find, carefully testing our surroundings for edible or useful resources. I was grateful for each chance to get out of the colony pod and into the woods, and I enjoyed my solitude amongst the strange, alien trees.

Sure, I wasn't supposed to be alone. Carrington wanted me to bring one of his sons along, but I valued my solitude too much for that. And, honestly, I felt safer with Crashland's wildlife than I did with David Carrington — the young man looked at me like I was some kind of prize to be won and I dreaded being alone with him.

He hadn't done anything. Not yet. And I didn't want to give him an opportunity. So when my turn came, I snuck off alone and took a rifle for protection.

Going armed was overkill. Henry ought to see off any Crashland wildlife with his ultrasound, projected from the special speakers on my wristband. Better safe than sorry, though, so I took the gun too.

Crashland's short day caught me by surprise, and when evening fell, I was still outside the ultrasonic fence. The light dimmed, the purple trees looming over me, their strange shadows adding to the unearthly ambience as I hurried back. If I didn't reach the pod by dark Carrington would demand an explanation. Worse, he might insist that his son accompany me everywhere from now on. That felt like a fate worse than death.

But something else worried me too. Something at the edge of my awareness. A feeling of being stalked, hunted. Had one of the big predators finally made its way here? I'd heard descriptions of monsters over the comms and thanked my lucky stars that none of them lived in our area.

I checked with Henry: according to him, the ultrasound was working fine, but of course I couldn't hear a thing. Maybe the speakers were broken? Henry still barked, but that didn't mean the higher frequencies that scared off animals were playing.

Worrying that my luck had run out, I glanced over my shoulder, shrinking from every shadow. The colony pod wasn't far now, but the light dimmed around me. I crossed the boundary of the ultrasonic fence and relaxed a little. None of the wildlife should be able to pass the posts, driven away by the sounds that no human could hear.

If there was a native predator behind me, I should be safe from it now. Rather than hurry home, I decided to take the time to see what was stalking me, if anything. Ducking behind a fallen tree, I turned to look back past the fence, expecting to find nothing. It had, I was certain, all been in my imagination.

I'd laugh at myself, go back to the pod, and get something to eat. Forget all about it until the next time I let my brain spook me. Yep.

Henry didn't share my optimism. He stared silently back into the forest, his teeth bared. An adorable puppy trying to look threatening, standing between me and harm. I blinked. *That* wasn't my imagination.

Maybe we'd both been spooked by nothing at all, but that seemed less likely. I strained my eyes, staring into the gathering dusk. Trees moved in the gentle wind, but I saw a hint of something else.

My rifle was slung over my shoulder and I lifted it

slowly, remembering the lessons. Easy to use, easy to aim. Bracing the stock against my shoulder, I aimed into the dusk and looked again, focusing where Henry pointed.

Someone was moving in the trees. In the dim light I barely saw them — wasn't sure I *had* seen them, in fact. I checked again and couldn't see anything now. But some instinct told me not to ignore the hologram's warning, and I put my finger on the trigger as I searched for my target. I only caught glimpses of whatever moved out there. A shadow moving in the darkness, following my trail.

Whatever it was, the shadow ignored the fencepost and crossed the invisible line no Crashland animal should be able to pass. My hands shook and I took a deep breath to steady myself. If it wasn't a native animal, then what was hunting me? One of the prytheen? That wasn't a comforting thought.

Had it seen me, too? I didn't know. Behind the fallen tree I was in pretty good cover, and the dim dusk light meant that everything blurred together. If I kept low and moved slowly, perhaps I'd get away unseen.

Maybe it's one of the Carringtons, I told myself. *Out hunting too late.* I didn't believe it for a second, though. Whatever I'd seen, it moved with a grace that was beyond any human I'd ever seen.

There! Something moved again, closer this time, heading towards the pod. I bit my lip, heart hammering in my chest, and eased off the safety. The rifle felt like a lead weight in my hands as I pointed it in the direction of the movement.

It *had* to be a prytheen, one of the alien attackers who'd forced us down on this planet. And that meant that we were in deadly danger. Fingers trembling, I looked down the sights and tried to make out my target through the strange, alien trees. Closer now, I caught glimpses of it. Something humanoid, blue-skinned, big but silent. Something *dangerous.*

It — he? — moved closer. Headed for the pod. For *Malcolm.* Undeniably alien, he moved with the easy grace of a hunting cat ready to pounce. And I would not let him pass. I couldn't. Leaning against the tree, I braced myself and sighted carefully. My finger took up the slack on the trigger and I squeezed.

The crack of the shot was loud in the quiet forest. The rifle slammed into my shoulder, the muzzle rose, and for a terrible moment I wondered what would happen if I'd missed my shot. But when I brought the sights down again, my target lay slumped against a tree.

I'd shot someone. My fingers shook as I stood and ran over to see who, what, I'd shot. I didn't know what to feel, what to think. *I had to do it,* I told myself. *He was hunting me.*

The alien lay against the tree where I'd shot him, hands clutching at his stomach and blue blood pulsing through his fingers. I looked down at him — tall, muscular, handsome in an inhuman way. Golden eyes looked back at me out of a rugged face, and his chest rose and fell as he breathed through sharp teeth. Even injured, he looked dangerous. Powerful. He wore a tight tunic and over it, webbing holding more knives than any one man had a right to.

He? Yes, he was definitely, undeniably male. I swallowed, lowering the rifle. He was no threat to me now. *What do I do now?*

The obvious answer was to call the pod and tell everyone. I should have done that right away, but the shock of seeing, of *shooting*, an alien had been too much for me. Fumbling to activate my wristband comm, I wondered what the other colonists would make of this.

Before I could make the call, I heard a branch snap behind me. Swinging around, bringing the rifle back up, I realized my mistake. Why the fuck had I thought there'd only be one of them?

I squeezed the trigger but a powerful hand grabbed the barrel and pushed it off line, sending the shot wide of my target. Another hand grabbed my throat, lifting me off the ground. I struggled, kicking and choking, the world going dark as I came face to face with an alien warrior's rage.

4

TORRAN

"Don't kill her!" The words were out of my mouth before I thought about them, snapped with all the force I could command. Arvid paused, looking around in surprise with the human female dangling from his hand. She thrashed helplessly, her pale face turning purple. Her rifle had fallen to the forest floor, leaving her defenseless.

"She shot you," Arvid said, shaking his head and squeezing tighter. Her hands clutched his wrist, pulling futilely.

I tried to stand, my strength failing me halfway. The pain hadn't reached me yet, but the icy cold of shock closed around me. Everything felt distant, slow, and focusing was hard — but some deep-seated part of me knew that I had to save the human.

"If anyone's going to kill her, it will be me," I said. Not the best argument, but the only one that came to mind. "She shot me; it's my right to take revenge."

Arvid shrugged and threw the human in my direction. She collapsed where she fell, clutching at her throat and gasping for air.

"Fair," Arvid said, picking up her rifle. "You take your revenge, we'll take the rest of the prey."

He vanished into the forest before I had a chance to reply, leaving me staring at the human. She was beautiful, face shining in the moonlight, green eyes flashing as she approached. She wore her hair long, unlike a prytheen female, and I yearned to run a hand through those dark locks.

If she was the last thing I saw, I'd die happy. A smile spread on my face despite the pain and the cold spreading through me from my wound.

You're in shock, I told myself. I ought to want her dead. She'd shot me, missed killing me by a fingerbreadth. Even now I might not make it — a gut wound was no easy thing to treat without proper medical technology. If my wound got infected, we'd have to rely on whatever medicine we could claim from the primitive human colony ship.

Training and tradition called out for revenge, urging me to send her into the lands of the dead ahead of me. But I knew that I wouldn't do it, that I couldn't harm her. The world faded, dimming as blood loss took its toll on me, and all I saw was her.

She watched me, her eyes wide, fingers twitching. Was she wrestling with the same feelings? Trying to kill me and escape had to be a tempting thought for her, but she didn't reach for my weapons. Good. If she'd tried, I'd have to defend myself and in my condition I might not be able to do that without hurting her.

Somewhere in the forest a shot rang out, then another. Human laser weapons followed by human screams. They might outnumber us but Arvid and the others were warriors of the Silver Band. These human colonists wouldn't stand a chance. I just hoped Arvid didn't need to kill any of them to capture our prize.

The female's gaze darted up at the sounds, and she scrambled back. Before she had the chance to stand and run into the darkness of the forest, I grabbed her wrist.

"No," I said in Galtrade, hoping that she spoke the language. Any spacefarer ought to, but these humans were new to the stars. "If you run, they will hunt you down. Kill you. Stay."

The strain of moving, of talking, made me shake. Coldness leeched into my bones, and I sat back hard. But I kept my grip on her arm, even as she tried to pull away from me. *Sundered Space, must I kill myself to protect her?*

Not that she would be safe if Arvid returned to find me dead and her alive. I grimaced at the thought, struggling to stay conscious as she tried to pull herself free. The world faded into nothing and the last thing I saw before the shadows claimed me was the sparkling green of her eyes.

Flickers of consciousness followed as I fought against the call of the healing trance. I needed to rest if I was to recover, but I would not let go of the world around me. Could not, until I knew what would happen to her.

Footsteps crushed fallen leaves underfoot, startling me back to consciousness. The cold, distant pain overwhelmed me, and I gasped in agony. Trying to move was too much; even listening strained my limited reserves of energy.

The human is still there, I thought dimly as I heard her speak. My hand gripped her wrist, holding on tight. *That's good.*

Whatever she said, I missed it. But not Arvid's reply.

"If he dies, you die," he snarled, and the human whimpered. Anger flared in me at that, burning in my blood. I tried to speak but the darkness closed around me again.

The next thing I knew, strong hands lifted and carried me. The slightest jolt sent searing pain through me, as though someone had touched a hot poker to my wound. My eyes wouldn't open, and though I heard voices around me, I couldn't make out the words. *Let me sleep,* I tried to say, but no sound came out.

After an excruciating journey, they lowered me onto a soft mattress. The relief as I stopped moving was immense, and I settled back into my healing trance.

Some time later, I had no idea how long, I woke to

feel gentle hands on my skin. Cool water bathed me, and a soft voice soothed in a language I didn't know.

My eyes flickered open for a moment and I saw the human female above me. Frightened but beautiful, she sang something quietly to herself as she cleaned my wound. A smile settled on my face and I relaxed back into the trance.

Everything was going to be alright.

∽

A STRANGE FEELING WOKE ME, like a warm rubbery sponge dragged across my face. My eyes opened to see a small mammal licking me, a ball of golden fluff that blocked my field of vision. A faint shimmer marked the creature as a hologram, but a forcefield gave it enough reality to touch me.

An odd but not unpleasant sensation, one which I did not have time for. I tried to sit, dislodging the virtual animal, only for a wave of dizziness to push me back into the bed. The fur ball bounced up onto my chest, licking my face enthusiastically again.

Generating the creature was a waste of computer cycles, but I couldn't help smiling. There was something endearing about the hologram, whatever its purpose.

"Get off," I said, cursing how weak my voice sounded. However long I'd been out it hadn't been enough time to recover from being shot.

"You're awake," someone said in strongly accented

Galtrade. I looked around, pushing the animal aside feebly, to see the human female who'd shot me watching warily from the far side of the room.

Room? Yes, I was no longer on the forest floor. Inside somewhere, a small room built to human scale — the bed I lay on wasn't quite long enough, and the ceiling looked painfully low. There were posters on the wall, slogans in a language I didn't recognize and primitive equipment that might be medical.

The door was shut, leaving me and the human alone together. My weapons and other gear sat on a table by the bed, and she stood as far away from them as possible.

In the bright electric light she looked frightened and pale. Her hands twitched as she backed against the wall, gaze darting from me to the door and back. This was the first chance I'd had to look at a human properly.

Small. Soft. Weak. No threat to a prytheen warrior. But there was something about her, a determination hidden beneath her fear, that made me certain she shouldn't be underestimated. And more than that, she was beautiful. Her pale skin looked soft, with curves I ached to run my hands over concealed under her jumpsuit. Pink skin rather than the blue of my people, exotic and tempting. I felt my body stir at the sight of her and growled, trying to contain a response I wasn't well enough to act on.

This isn't the time or place, I told myself. *Information, that's what I need, not a female.*

"How long have I been out?" I asked.

"Three days," she answered. Her accent was awful but at least we could communicate. That was a good start.

I tried to sit up, slower this time, and managed to prop myself against the wall. The room swam around me and I groaned at the effort. Three days hadn't been enough time for the healing trance to fix my injury, not by a long way.

I focused on the human female, steadying myself as I looked at her. Oddly, her presence made me feel better — though I couldn't forget that she was the one who'd put me in this position.

Her pale face flushed as I watched her, and she looked away. Her blush was delightful and I smiled despite myself. Not wanting to frighten her, I looked away with difficulty.

"My name is Torran," I told her, speaking slowly and trying to keep my pain from showing in my voice. I doubted that I'd been successful. "What is yours?"

"Lisa," she said. Her gaze darted up to me, a complicated mix of emotions crossing her face too fast for me to follow.

"What happened?" I asked, needing to understand. Her gaze hardened as she bit her lip, and I saw both anger and fear in her eyes before she looked away.

"Your people attacked us, took us prisoner," she said. "Arvid says this is their place now, that we are theirs. Yours too, I suppose. And I'm to tend your wounds since I…"

She trailed off, perhaps not wanting to remind me that she'd shot me. As though I could forget such a thing. I grunted and tried to think clearly. What she'd told me made sense, but it wasn't exactly good news. Conquering a lesser race was against our Code and breaking it left a bad taste in my mouth. On the other hand, what were we supposed to do? The humans' technology worked and ours did not: we needed their colony.

Still, part of me regretted leading Arvid here. If I'd chosen a different course I would never have heard the high-pitched sound of the humans' defenses, never tracked them to their home. Perhaps, had I gone another way, we'd have found other prytheen instead of the humans.

What's past is done, I told myself. *Move forward, not back.* We'd found humans, and that was that. But from the fear in the human's expression, I doubted that Arvid was handling the situation well. With a growl, I tried to stand. I got half-way off the bed before my knees gave way, and I barely caught myself. Hauling myself back onto the bed, I lay back and took a deep, frustrated breath.

Fine. If I couldn't go see Arvid, he would have to come to me.

"Tell Arvid I am awake."

She hesitated. My jaw tightened and I brimmed with anger. Anger at Arvid rather than her. *She tried to kill me; why do I care if she's afraid?*

"I will not let him hurt you," I promised when she

didn't move. It didn't seem to convince her, so I growled. "Must I fetch him myself?"

With a grunt of effort I began to pull myself to my feet again. *That* spurred her into action — she put her hand on my chest and pushed me back down, a worried look on her face.

The touch of her hand on my bare skin sent a strange sensation through me. As though a pulse of fire burned along my nerves. Not painful. The reverse, in fact. I nearly didn't hear her speak over my surprise at the sensation.

What is this feeling?

"I will fetch him," she said, stumbling over her words. "Don't… you just stay put. Yes?"

I nodded. That was all I'd been asking for, though part of me didn't want her to leave my presence. Sinking back into the soft mattress, I shut my eyes. Just for a moment.

The door slamming open shocked me back to consciousness. I grabbed for a knife before remembering it wasn't at my belt.

"Torran, you live!" Arvid strode into the small room, voice booming loud enough to make me wince. "I wasn't sure you'd make it."

"I have had good care," I said, stretching a little and wincing. "Though I will need longer to recuperate."

"The little human's been doing her best. No wonder: I told her she lives only as long as you do." Arvid laughed and I hid my angry response.

"She did fine work for an alien," I told him. "Now what?"

Arvid's grin faded. "That's not an easy question. It seems that we're trapped here, all of us — the human ship is a wreck too. And it's in the hands of a human captain. Zaren's dead."

I closed my eyes and tried to take that in. The leader who'd taken us on this doomed attack, the Alpha-Captain who'd gotten us stranded here, was dead? My instinct was to applaud, but without him to hold the Silver Band together we were certain to fall into infighting and chaos.

Arvid laid out what had happened at the *Wandering Star* quickly, and it was as bad as I'd feared. Zaren dead, Auric ruling along with the human captain. The Silver Band dissolving into squabbling clans around the planet. No one had heard from Terasi, my Alpha-Captain, and it wasn't even clear she was on Crashland.

I hoped that she wasn't. Someone had to lead whatever remained of the Silver Band outside of this accursed system, and better her than most. But it left me with no one to turn to for advice or leadership.

"Still, we're well situated," Arvid finished with forced cheer. "These humans have a good thing going — plentiful hunting, good shelter, the beginnings of a farm. And now we have them to do the work for us while you and Dessus recover from your wounds."

My lips twitched. Enslaving the humans to work the farm they'd set up? There was no honor in that. But I wasn't in a position to challenge Arvid for leadership of our tiny clan, and if Dessus and Tarva backed him, there was nothing I could do. Not until I had healed, at least.

He took my silence for agreement and bulled on. "There are other survivors. We will regroup eventually, but for now we must consolidate our position. And that means leaving no doubt what happens if one of the humans raises a hand against us, Torran."

I saw where this was going and glared up at him. "She is my prey, Arvid, not yours to do with as you please."

"Sundered Space, Torran, I know that." Arvid's impatience showed through. "She shot you, you get to deal with her. Now you're conscious, we can proceed with the execution."

I bared my teeth and glared at him, fingers tensing and claws sliding from their sheathes. Arvid might be healthy and armed but my instincts didn't care about those details.

Why does it matter so much? She shot me, what do I care if she lives or dies?

It made no sense. It didn't have to. I just knew that I would kill anyone who laid a finger on her.

"No," I said, forcing myself to sound calm. If I let out my anger, I didn't know how far I'd go. "Without her help I wouldn't have survived this far. I owe her for that."

"You owe her for the gut wound that nearly killed you, Torran." Arvid spoke slowly, carefully. The room felt too small for the two of us, and we both knew that if a fight broke out, it would be a disaster — he kept his hands clear of his weapons, unthreatening. "We cannot let the humans think they can attack us and live. There are more of them than us, and both you and Dessus still need to heal. Tarva and I can't keep the others under watch constantly."

I growled but forced my hands to relax. Killing Arvid wouldn't help me, or Lisa, or anyone else. And in my present state I doubted I'd survive a fight with him either.

But that didn't mean I'd give in. "She lives. You've acknowledged that she's my prey, Arvid, and this is my decision. If any of the other humans are stupid enough to think it gives them leave to attack a prytheen, we'll soon teach them better."

Arvid snorted at that, and I knew what he thought. If the humans rose up against us as one, then the two healthy prytheen warriors might not be enough to put them down. *Well, that's his problem to deal with,* I thought. *He's the one who wanted to conquer.*

"If you claim her, then I can't argue," he said after a long, heavy pause. "The Code backs you on this, I know. But it means you have to keep her in line. She's your responsibility."

Unhappy but willing to go along with it. That was the best I'd been able to hope for out of this exchange. I nodded, not entirely happy myself. A compromise.

Tension left Arvid's shoulders and I relaxed back into the bed.

"I don't envy our leaders," he said, smiling a little.

"Juggling problems like this every day must wear on a man. I'm glad I won't be in charge here for long, Torran."

"How's that? Who else can take over?" I knew Tarva didn't want the job any more than I did, and Dessus made a better follower than a leader. Of the four of us, Arvid was the closest thing to a leader.

"I told you there are other survivors," he said. "Dessus managed to get one of our transmitters working, powered by the humans' communicator, and we've found friends. Some of Zaren's clan are nearby and we need their numbers. This place gives us wealth enough to buy our way in near the top, whoever ends up as the clan's Alpha-Captain now that Zaren's gone into the dark."

I groaned. The clan that had led us on this fool's attack? But the sheer relief in Arvid's eyes at the thought of no longer being in charge made one thing clear — he wasn't going to be the boss any longer than he had to.

And I wasn't up to challenging him for the position, not yet. Perhaps by the time our new 'friends' arrived, I'd be on my feet and able to take charge.

Or perhaps they would prove more reasonable than their dead leader had been. I could hope, though it didn't seem likely.

"Let me rest and heal," I told Arvid. "I'd rather be up and around by the time Zaren's people arrive."

He nodded and turned to leave. As soon as he was out of the room, I realized how much the conversation had taken out of me. My wound burned and keeping my eyes open was impossible. The healing trance wouldn't be enough to deal with this, and I had to hope that the humans' primitive technology could help me fight off whatever infection was setting in.

5

LISA

The sickbay door slid shut behind me and I leaned against the wall, glad to be out of there. The small room felt crowded when Torran was unconscious — as soon as he'd stirred, I'd felt trapped with him.

Oddly, it wasn't an entirely unwelcome feeling. We were too close together, there wasn't enough space, and I should have been terrified of him. An alien warrior I'd shot, and plenty of weapons if he wanted revenge.

Not that he'd need them. Even injured he seemed strong enough to do whatever he wanted if he got his hands on me.

My cheeks heated at the thought and I frowned, banishing an image of those powerful blue hands pulling me close. *What the hell, Lisa? Is this some kind of Stockholm syndrome bullshit?*

Torran was undeniably sexy, with a muscular body

that put every human I'd ever seen to shame. I swallowed and shook my head, trying to focus on what he and Arvid were saying rather than drifting into ridiculous flights of fancy. Even if I'd actually been interested in him, I'd *shot* him.

The two aliens spoke loudly enough that I could hear most of what they said, but it didn't help. My Galtrade wasn't bad and since our capture I'd been working hard to improve along with my fellow humans — being able to understand our alien overlords made everything easier. It helped that Galtrade was designed to be easy to learn.

But the language the prytheen spoke amongst themselves was different, harder to grasp, and they didn't try to teach it to us. I sighed, giving up on eavesdropping.

Either they'll decide to kill you now or not, I told myself. *There's nothing I can do about it. Might as well take the chance to see the others.*

I pushed away from the wall, turning my back on the tiny sickbay. On Arcadia there would have been flying ambulances to take the seriously injured to the *Wandering Star* for treatment, but here on Crashland who knew if we'd ever have a luxury like that?

Outside, our small farm had taken shape. Trees cut down and rolled aside, the resulting space planted with crops. Not enough to feed us all, of course. Clearing that much forest would take time — but it was a good start.

Hard work, though, and the other colonists were

doing the backbreaking labor of getting it set up. Even with modern tools, cutting down and mulching up the trees to free the soil for crops was hard going. Mr. Carrington insisted he was still in charge, of course, though he left the Dietrichs to do most of the technical work. When I emerged from the pod the others gathered by a fallen tree, Maria Dietrich setting up the nanotech that would consume the stump while the Carrington boys moved the log to the side.

I looked past them into the woods, wondering if I should just walk into them and hope I found somewhere better. But that would be suicide — aside from the fact that I had no supplies for a journey, the Crashland's predators would eat me alive. One of the first things Arvid had done to establish his control was disable the ultrasound speakers on our wristbands. I'd have no protection from predators, even if the prytheen didn't hunt me down.

Mr. Carrington spotted me standing in the pod's doorway and coughed to get my attention.

"I see you've decided to join us, Lisa," he said. "Perhaps you can pull your weight for once. Your brother is worse than useless."

My pulse quickened at that and I barely restrained my urge to snap back at him. His style of 'leadership' only inspired anger in me, especially when it looked like he'd done no work himself. Of all the humans out here, he was the only one who'd kept clean and tidy.

The remaining two prytheen watched with amused interest as he glared at me and I restrained my impulse to shout back. We humans had to stick together, I told myself, but that wasn't always easy.

"I can't work out here and tend the sickbay," I pointed out as reasonably as I could manage, trying for a smile and hoping it didn't come across as hostile as I felt. Carrington snorted but I pressed on. "What do you think the aliens will do if the one we injured dies? Do you think they'll just be angry at me?"

"Why not?" Carrington asked, venom in his voice. "You're the one who shot him."

"She's right, Mr. Carrington," Maria said, not taking her eyes off her computer interface. The holographic monkey sat on the offending tree stump, directing the nanites as they worked their way into the wood. "We're all better off if he lives."

Carrington muttered something under his breath, and I knew I hadn't heard the last of his complaints. But for now he shut up, turning to direct the boys as they stripped branches from the fallen tree. Those would be fed into the matter processor and used to make nutrient paste.

It wasn't good food, and it wouldn't sustain life forever, but it was what we had. Now that the prytheen had taken over, they reserved the hunted meat for themselves.

"Thank you for backing me up," I said quietly to Maria as I joined her. She finished programming the nanites and set them to work before turning to me.

"I know Carrington's type, he needs to be in

charge," she said, just as quiet. "As long as we give him that, he'll stay out of our way."

Next to us the stump steamed as tiny machines burrowed into it. Over the next days they'd make their way into the roots, tearing up everything and mulching it until it was food for worms.

That felt like a metaphor for my life. All my hopes and dreams were being ground up to support someone else's.

"What do we do past that?" I asked, and she shrugged, surrendering to fate.

"We do what the conquered always do. We adapt, survive, look for ways to improve things. All of us are better off if the farm runs well, so I will make the best farm I can. And as long as Carrington is content to pretend to be in charge rather than interfering, I can make it happen."

Fuck that. I restrained myself from saying it out loud, but there had to be a better way forward. Maria might be willing to surrender to the aliens, but I wouldn't. I *couldn't*.

There was no point in fighting about it here though, not with two aliens watching and Carrington close enough to overhear. I sighed and put off any thought of resistance for the time being — there would be a better chance. There *had to be* a better chance.

"Show me how to do this?" I asked, looking for safer ground. Learning how to use the tech might be useful. Maria smiled.

"Of course. It's easy to do, tricky to do well," she

told me. "The machines must be carefully programmed or we will waste them, and we do not have as many as we need."

That was certainly true. The nanites we'd packed on the colony pod were an expensive tool, and impossible to replace on Crashland. Oh, somewhere someone might have a breeder system that made more of the tiny machines, but not us. When we ran out, we'd have to dig up tree stumps by hand and that didn't sound like fun given how many we'd need to clear.

Maria showed me the tricks she'd developed to make do with as few nanites as possible, and I copied her custom programming over to Henry who barked excitedly at his new job. I wondered just how many programs I could load into his little AI. Between the medical texts and the nanite controls, his storage matrix was getting full.

But anything that made me more useful would be good. As soon as Torran was back on his feet I'd have to justify my existence. Hopefully that day wouldn't come too soon.

~

DAYS PASSED, most of them spent inside looking after Torran. He spent most of that time asleep or unconscious. Whatever infection ravaged his system kept him from waking, and I struggled to help him.

Maybe I should have spent more time helping the others clear the forest but every time I thought I could spare the effort, something changed for the worse. Torran's fever spiked, an infection bloomed, his wound wept, and I had to struggle dealing with it.

It didn't help that the autodoc didn't understand a prytheen body. Torran's vital signs made no sense, and poor Henry's programming kept giving contradictory advice until I switched off the error messages and started guessing what to do. The universal antibiotics worked their magic, but his prytheen metabolism reacted weirdly to something in them. And then the infection came back.

"I don't know what to do," I admitted to Henry eventually. He was meant to be a confidant, so I might as well use that function. He looked up at me with his gigantic eyes and somehow that comforted me.

Padding forward, he bumped his head against my arm, and I realized he'd updated his appearance: my holo-puppy had a holographic stethoscope draped around his fuzzy neck. I snorted laughter at the sight, and he headbutted me again.

"Okay, that doesn't actually help, but I feel a bit better," I said, scratching him behind the ears. "Let's see what we can get the autodoc to do."

Whether I had anything to do with it or not, over time Torran's condition slowly improved. Or at least settled — it was hard to say when I didn't know what his vital signs ought to look like. But he seemed to rest easier, and woke occasionally. I hoped it was a good sign. I didn't want to lose him, and not just because Arvid would kill me if he died.

Just as I started to think I had the situation under control, more prytheen arrived. I'd relaxed enough to take short breaks outside each day, and I happened to be outside with Malcolm when they showed up.

They filed out of the forest, battered and injured, looking around with hungry, desperate eyes. Unlike the first prytheen attackers, I heard these aliens approach before they arrived: they lacked Torran's silent grace in the woods. I counted twenty of them, more or less, and swallowed nervously. That was a lot of extra aliens.

The journey here hadn't treated them well — more than one had injuries too fresh to have been from the crash. The Crashland wildlife had taken its toll.

Arvid greeted the newcomers with formal words that meant nothing to us humans, but one of the new arrivals stepped forward and grasped his wrists in an alien handshake. He was the biggest of the new arrivals, and the only one who looked well-fed. A nasty scar ran from his face down his neck and vanished under the tight black uniform he wore.

It clung to his muscular body, showing off his perfectly defined abs, and the bulging muscles of his arms flexed as he gripped Arvid's hand. He looked formidable, almost as powerfully built as Torran. But where Torran's presence sent a flood of confused emotions through me, this new alien simply frightened me.

The cruelty in his eyes as he looked at us chilled my

soul. Maybe I imagined it? I hoped so, because this man was clearly in charge now.

The new aliens growled and snarled and Arvid turned to Mr. Carrington, switching to Galtrade. "You, bring food for our guest."

The way Carrington jumped to obey, I almost expected him to salute. I ground my teeth, trying to be fair. The man had a family to think about, the lives of three children on the line. He had no choice here.

It still didn't look good, the way he scurried off to do our alien masters' bidding. I tried not to think about it

"You are the one who shot a prytheen?" The new alien's voice was as rough as his face, dark and dangerous. Half a smile tugged at his lips, exposing sharp teeth.

I gulped and nodded quickly, hoping he'd lose interest. His eyes narrowed.

"Why do you let her live?" He directed the question to Arvid, not me, but he stuck to Galtrade. Probably to frighten me, I thought, and if so, it worked. I shivered as the other alien explained.

"Torran has claimed her, Gurral. She's his to kill or spare."

Gurral looked me over again, eyes flicking up and down my body as though assessing a side of beef. Something sparked in his eyes, anger or lust I couldn't tell. It didn't matter; both options terrified me.

"As long as he's alive, anyway," the alien said, reaching out to brush my cheek with his finger. I resisted the urge to slap his hand away. That wouldn't help anything.

Our eyes met and we measured each other. I saw the cold hardness of his will, a cruelty and darkness I didn't want to test.

Torran, you'd better get well soon, I thought as I looked down, trying to appear meek and passive and unthreatening. *If you die on me, I won't live long.*

If Gurral tried anything with me I had no illusions about what would happen. I'd fight him and die. Maybe, with a lot of luck, I'd kill him on my way out.

Gurral grinned, a nasty expression that made me shiver. Turning back to his men he started to give orders, and I took the chance to vanish back to sickbay and get out of sight. The less he saw of me, the better.

It wasn't that easy, of course. Now that Torran didn't need constant care and attention, the aliens weren't about to let me hide myself away, especially when we needed more farmland than ever. Feeding all our new prytheen guests would take a lot more land than we'd planned on, and they couldn't live by hunting alone.

Getting the farmland expanded was only the first problem — tending the crops would be a lot of work, even with the genetically engineered super-crops we'd brought.

It would have been a lot easier if the aliens helped, but no. They were content to watch us work, 'encouraging' their human slaves. That worked to an extent:

none of us wanted to find out what they'd do if they thought we weren't working hard enough.

To be completely fair, they did some work — just not on the farm. But all of the prytheen were happy to hunt in the forests, and while they didn't share any of the meat they brought home, that kept them from draining our supplies as quickly as they might have. And, perhaps more importantly, it meant that each day there were less of them hanging around the colony. Always one or two, keeping watch on us humans, but the rest vanished to hunt.

That was definitely better than having the crowd of them staring at us as we chopped down trees and cleared ground. A few days in and the routine seemed almost natural. But the aliens never let us forget who was in charge.

"You. Boy." The alien's words were harsh, brutal, uncaring. I glanced up from my work gathering chopped branches for the matter processor to see one of the prytheen glaring at Malcolm. My brother stood wearily, the pain of long hours working to clear the new fields showing in his tired stance.

"Fetch me a drink," the alien said, lounging against the side of the colony pod and watching us. Malcolm's eyes darted from him to the pod and back, and I prayed he wouldn't say something stupid. Which, really, would be anything the prytheen could understand.

"Fetch it yourself, you lazy ass." My heart nearly stopped, but at least Malcolm said it in Spanish. The aliens spoke Galtrade with us, and some of them were picking up a bit of English. Anything else was as mysterious to them as the prytheen language was to us.

The alien's eyes narrowed and he straightened up. He might not have understood the words, but I had the sinking feeling he knew why Malcolm had chosen a language he didn't speak. As my brother made his way to the pod, the prytheen stepped into his way.

I tried to think of something to say to stop the looming confrontation, but my mind moved too slowly and things happened fast. Malcolm looked up at the prytheen warrior, tried to step around him. The alien snarled something wordless and backhanded him hard enough to send him tumbling to the ground.

"Speak with respect," he said, kicking my brother as he started to stand. The impact drove the air out of Malcolm, leaving him gasping and quivering on the hard soil. The alien rained blows down on him, demanding an apology that Malcolm couldn't get out through the pain.

If no one stopped him, the alien would beat Malcolm to death. I felt it in my bones, and my body reacted while I was still trying to think of how to intervene.

"Stop it!" Before I knew what I was doing, I'd leaped onto the back of the prytheen warrior. My hands battered at his ears and he roared in surprise and confusion.

The element of surprise carried me for a moment, and I had a heady second where I thought I might achieve something. But then he grabbed me, claws digging into my shoulder, and threw me off him. I twisted in the air, trying to control my fall, and then the ground hit me hard.

Malcolm struggled up to his feet, taking the chance to run for the pod, but the prytheen wasn't about to be distracted from him. Lashing out with a kick, the alien monster sent my brother tumbling to the ground.

"Dead," he hissed, drawing a dagger and raising it over Malcolm. I scrambled to my feet, feeling like I was moving through treacle as I rushed towards them, and flung myself in the blade's path.

Everything seemed to move so slowly, and I could see every detail. Some strange insect flying past. The glint of the sun on the wickedly sharp dagger. The sound of my heart pounding in my ears as he swung it down.

Above us the sky shone blue. It was a beautiful day to die.

And then a hand caught the alien's wrist. A blue hand, a prytheen hand.

Torran's hand.

The blade halted inches from my face, and it was all I could look at. The tip shone bright — almost beautiful — poised to take my life or my brother's, and pulling my focus away was impossible.

Torran said something, hard words rough and angry in his throat. The other prytheen hissed a response, pulling his arm free and stepping back. My paralysis broke and I sucked in air as he sheathed his blade and glowered.

The anger in those eyes told me I hadn't heard the last of this, but he seemed content to turn away and stalk off. Malcolm pulled himself to his feet behind me, wincing and trembling. Torran looked down at the two of us. For a long breath none of us said anything.

To my surprise, I was the one to break the silence. "What the fuck are you doing out of bed?"

It was a ridiculous complaint. Even as I said it I knew it. He'd saved my life, probably Malcolm's too, and his reward was a telling-off? But my emotions were too complicated, too raw, to keep in check and they boiled out as anger.

It was safer than fear, which would have had me curl up into a ball and never come out.

"I told you to stay put, I told you that your wound'll reopen if you aren't careful. I don't want all my work to go to waste!"

Torran grunted something, annoyance or amusement. Shaking his head, he leaned back against the colony pod and let me shout. My eyes widened as I saw the dark marks on the bandage around his waist. He *had* torn his wound open. God damn it.

"Sis—" Malcolm said, and I wheeled on him before he could get anywhere.

"Don't you start," I told him, struggling to keep my voice down. "You nearly got yourself killed. Why didn't you just do what he said, you idiot? I can't let you die."

There were tears in my brother's eyes and his arms closed around me in a fierce hug. Sobs shook him and my anger drained away as fast as it appeared. I hugged

Malcolm hard, holding him and trying to give him the comfort I lacked.

"We have to be careful," I told him quietly, once I thought he might listen. "You're all I have left, you can't get yourself killed. Okay?"

"I'll be careful, sis," he said, choking the words out through sobs. "I promise."

He meant it. In the moment, at least, he meant it. But I knew my hot-headed brother too well — sooner or later, he'd get an idea in his head again and next time I might not be there to save him. Tears welled in my eyes again, and I pulled Malcolm close so he wouldn't see.

A strong hand landed on my shoulder, squeezing. Torran's touch should have been frightening, but it wasn't. Somehow it offered me the comfort I needed and the dread filling me faded.

Torran didn't talk, didn't need to. His touch offered me the support and understanding I needed in that moment.

But that's not enough. Thanks to him I could think clearly, and that wasn't comforting. *He won't be around all the time to protect me, or Malcolm. Sooner or later we're going to get ourselves killed, and maybe Torran will avenge us but that won't be much comfort to our corpses.*

Having an alien on our side might help, but it wasn't enough to make this place safe. If I wanted to save my brother, we had to escape.

6

TORRAN

Fate had been kind. If I hadn't chosen that moment to stretch my legs, Lisa would have died on Myrok's blade, and her brother too. That thought shook me far more than it had any reason to.

It's the infection, I told myself as I carefully leaned against the wall. *That's all. I'm part delirious.*

I knew it was a lie. My feelings for the human female were stronger than I let myself admit. She turned away from her brother, looked up at me, and I saw the mix of helpless anger and fear in her eyes. And something else hidden beneath them. I wasn't the only one unable to face what I really felt.

"You must rest," she said, trying to be stern. I nodded. There was no need to fight, and no use arguing. But when I took a step towards the colony pod, I stumbled and nearly fell.

The confrontation had taken more out of me than I'd realized.

Before I could steady myself, Lisa was there, an arm around my waist and her shoulder under my arm. Supporting me, helping me. My weight would be too much for her, I realized instantly, but her touch gave me strength and together we staggered inside.

Myrok lurked somewhere in the pod, but he kept out of the way. Good. I had no time for him or his dishonorable behavior. Preying on the weak and defenseless was no way for a warrior to behave.

Unfortunately that seemed to be what we'd been reduced to. I tried not to think about that too much as Lisa lowered me carefully back onto the sickbay bed and let the autodoc examine my injury again.

"Your fever's up," she said, worried, her little hologram padding over my chest as it ran the scan. "You really shouldn't have gotten out of bed."

"I will get up when I choose," I told her. No need to point out that she'd be dead if I hadn't — we both knew that.

A quick smile flashed across her face, there and gone so fast I'd have missed it if I blinked. "It's not like I can tie you down."

I nodded and lay back, letting her give me another shot. This time when she finished with the spray hypo, Lisa dropped it into her pocket rather than putting it back on the shelf. I frowned: I'd never seen her do that before.

You've been unconscious for most of your treatment. It could be perfectly innocent.

But I knew it wasn't. Her guilt showed in her

studied look of innocence, the way she immediately started to busy herself with something else. As though to distract me from what she'd done.

I wanted to tell her she wasn't good at this, whatever subterfuge she had planned. That she would only get herself killed if she tried something stupid. But the shot was taking effect and my strength drained from my muscles.

My worries faded too, the drugs leaving me sleepy and happy. I smiled up at Lisa and saw her smile again in response. That was all I needed to drift off in a happy slumber.

~

MY TRANCE KEPT me under for a full day before I woke again, this time with less pain to distract me. The injury was finally closing under the bandage, and my strength would return soon. Good. I would need it, now that Gurral and his warriors were here.

Long training and practice kept me from showing my recovery before I had to. I let myself come to consciousness without opening my eyes or speeding my breathing — a scout never knew when he might wake up in danger, especially from a healing trance that deep.

That shouldn't apply when I was in a safe place though. Something had made my subconscious class the sickbay as unsafe, and as I woke I tried to pinpoint what it was.

I heard quiet, surreptitious movement in the room. Sometimes trying to keep quiet sounded more suspicious than moving normally. Like an absence of noise where there ought to be sound, it drew my attention.

Slowly, carefully, I opened my eyes a crack and looked. There was Lisa, quietly loading medical supplies into a rucksack. My first thought was some kind of emergency, but that made no sense — she wouldn't be trying to keep quiet if that were the case.

No, she was stealing. The way she moved, her nervous glances at the door, made me certain. But why?

Because Gurral wouldn't waste valuable medical supplies on humans, I thought. That stung. The supplies had belonged to the humans until we took over, and now that Arvid had given command over to Gurral things were going from bad to worse for them. If Lisa had to steal medical supplies to help her fellow humans, I would not judge her for it.

But the others would. Someone moved in the corridor outside the small room, coming closer. A prytheen warrior, I could tell that much from his quiet stride. He was almost at the sickbay door.

Whoever it was, he moved quietly enough that Lisa's human senses hadn't noticed him approach. I didn't know what punishment Gurral would dish out to a human stealing medical supplies, and I had no intention of finding out.

Groaning, I stirred theatrically and sat up. Lisa gasped, a little strangled yelp of a sound that would have been funny in other circumstances, and dropped her bag as she turned towards me. It was hard to pretend I hadn't noticed the thump of it hitting the floor, or the terror in her eyes as she kicked it out of sight, but I managed.

"You're awake," she exclaimed, then caught her breath and managed an unconvincing smile. "That's... good."

Before I needed to reply, the door slid open and Gurral stepped in. Lisa froze, looking like she wanted to vanish into the floor.

"What do you want, Gurral?" I asked, drawing his attention away from her. "I'm injured and I need my rest."

"Not too injured to pick a fight with one of my men," he said, grinning. The expression didn't reach his eyes. "Myrok tells me you threatened to kill him over a human."

I felt my fingers tense, claws sliding out of their sheathes before I could stop myself. "The human is mine. Claimed. He had no right to harm her."

Gurral cocked his head to one side, looked at Lisa and then at me. Nodded once, a carefully measured expression. It would be easy to dismiss the man as a brute, a thug, but I saw through that to what lay beneath. He had the cunning and patience to be dangerous in the way a simple monster would never be.

A leader to be careful around, at least until I'd recovered from my injuries. He would make a strong leader for this growing clan, but that wasn't necessarily a good thing.

"I'll not take a warrior's prey from him," he said, carefully watching my reaction. "Nor will I let a human disrespect one of us. When you have recovered, you will be the one to slay her for her actions. In front of everyone, to make certain the humans understand that they cannot hide behind one warrior for protection from another."

And so that the prytheen know you can control me, I added silently. I took a breath, thinking before I spoke again. If I was going to avoid his demand that I kill Lisa, I needed a good excuse. Only one excuse came to mind.

"She is more than just my prey. She is my khara." I'd intended that to be a lie, but as soon as the words left my lips, I knew it wasn't. My heart thumped in my chest, so loud I thought even a human would hear it. It took all my discipline to not look around at her, but I *felt* her in the room beside me. Her presence gave me confidence and strength, and I realized I'd been hiding this from myself from the moment we met.

From the moment she shot me, I reminded myself, amused at the thought. I'd laid eyes on the love of my life and her reaction had been to put a laser bolt through my body.

Gurral watched me, weighing my words and judging me. His scarred face hid his emotions well, though a growing anger leaked through. "Your khara? That seems… unlikely, Torran."

The crowning irony would be if he didn't believe my 'lie' now I'd realized it was the truth. If the stakes hadn't been so high, I would have laughed. Instead, I met Gurral's gaze with a deadly stare, daring him to argue.

"There have been other mated pairs who fought each other," I reminded him. "In the old ballads—"

"Oh yes, the *old ballads* tell of many things," he said, sneering. "Giant space beasts, god-like energy beings, love that spans centuries. I don't put too much stock in those tales."

I shrugged. "Very well. You do not have to believe them. Just me."

We looked at each other long enough that I wondered if I'd overplayed my hand. If he pushed it, I'd have to fight him, and though my injury was healing it would be long days before I was back to full strength.

On the other hand, Gurral had much to lose by appearing weak. If he attacked me now, still on my hospital bed, his warriors would see him as a coward.

His lip twitched, showing an emotion I couldn't read before he hid it behind his perpetual sneer.

"Zaren doubted that humans could be our kharas," he said carefully. "And that was the death of him. I shall not make his mistake, so I offer you my congratulations."

I let out a breath. But Gurral wasn't finished yet. "It will be your responsibility to keep your human out of trouble, though. Khara or not, she took her life in her hands challenging Myrok — if you do not keep her under control, you will have to answer for her mistakes."

"I will make sure she understands," I rumbled. It was the best compromise I could hope for. Far more reasonable than I'd expected from Gurral, and I trusted neither him nor it. "Soon I will be able to pull my weight again, and I will make amends to Myrok."

"Good," Gurral said, offering me his arm. We clasped wrists as though we were old friends, and his fingers dug into my arm. Testing my strength, asserting his dominance. I met his eyes and squeezed back.

His eyes narrowed, hiding a wince, and I relaxed. Good. He wouldn't take me for easy prey. But if he saw me as a rival that might be even worse. I had a fine line to walk, doom waiting if I made a single misstep.

"We need your skills," Gurral said. "Terasi trusted you, which is all the recommendation I need. Now she's gone and I need you to scout for me. This farm is a good start but we must gather more humans if we are to feed our people and build up a secure base. And this planet is dangerous — finding a safe route to their settlements will not be an easy task. I lost warriors on the journey here and do not intend to lose more if I can help it."

Ah. So that's what he wants from me. It would have been easy for him to kill me and appease his follower, but if he had a use for my skills, he wouldn't waste them. Gurral planned ahead, which made him more dangerous than some random warlord. But it also gave me some security, a path to acceptance in his new clan.

As long as I helped him and didn't threaten his leadership, I would be safe and so would Lisa. That was tempting even if the price was to hunt fresh slaves for his workforce.

"The wildlife is dangerous, especially without equipment to deal with it," I said cautiously, nodding. "Traveling any distance has its risks. But I can find a way — if we know where to find the humans."

Gurral's smile broadened. "That's not a problem, not with the communication equipment here. The humans are gathering into their own communities, and some of those are close enough to reach."

And of course the colony pods communicated with each other. The humans might come to regret that feature of their technology.

"I will be fit to scout soon," I told Gurral, hiding my reluctance behind my genuine excitement at getting back to hunting. Tracking down human communities to raid wasn't what I had in mind, and his cunning eyes looked deep into my soul, searching for signs of deceit. I didn't know how long I'd be able to keep him fooled.

For today, though, I'd passed his test. With a nod, Gurral turned and stalked out of the room as quietly as he'd entered. Did the man sneak everywhere? The door slid shut behind him and Lisa and I were alone once more.

She let out a long, shuddering breath and sat back against the counter. Her face had gone white as cometary ice, and even now her eyes were fixed on the door. When I reached out a hand to touch her shoulder, she flinched back as though she'd forgotten I was in the room.

"You are safe," I told her. "I will protect you."

"Why?" Lisa asked, her voice shaking. "Why are you protecting me? I *shot* you, I nearly killed you."

My laugh surprised me almost as much as it did her. "Should I hold that against you? You were defending yourself against an attacker, and I respect that even if the attacker was me."

"Besides, you missed."

That was enough to make her glare, color returning to her face as her cheeks heated. Her look of outrage just made her cuter.

"I *did not* miss," she objected. "If I had, I wouldn't have been stuck here tending your damned wound."

"You missed everything vital," I corrected myself. "If you had a prytheen medical system here I'd be fully recovered by now."

"If we had a prytheen medical system it wouldn't work any better than the rest of your technology. You're damned lucky any of the medicine we have can help, and that Henry here has a good biology database."

Her virtual companion appeared, a ball of golden fur that bounced happily as she scratched behind its ears. It might be an absurd interface but I couldn't help smiling at the sight, and it did seem to relax her.

I nodded, conceding her point. "In that case I owe you and Henry a debt for saving my life. Let me repay it by taking care of you."

Telling her about the khara bond that joined us

would be complicated, and this wasn't the time or place. That's what I told myself anyway, though I wondered when the time would be right. Was this simply an excuse to put it off?

No, Lisa's life had been upended too many times in the past days. Telling her that she was my mate, that fate had chosen us for each other, that might be too much for her. She was near her breaking point already, and I couldn't afford to scare her away. Not when I was all that kept her safe from the other prytheen.

"I'd better go," she said after a pause, lifting my hand from her shoulder. I saw the reluctance in her eyes and almost smiled — she wanted to be near me as much as I wanted her company. But she had other duties and I needed my rest. If she stayed in arm's reach I doubted I'd be able to restrain myself.

So I nodded. "Go, but be careful. Myrok is angry, and he will take that out on you if he gets the chance."

7

LISA

*O*ut of sickbay, safely away from Torran, I stopped to get my emotions under control. Fear and relief flooded through me leaving me a trembling mess.

Why did Torran have to wake up in the middle of the night? Why had Gurral chosen that moment to visit him? I'd chosen my time carefully, the middle of the night when everyone ought to be asleep.

Just bad luck, I told myself, squeezing my eyes shut and trying not to give in to panic. *Neither of them knows you're trying to escape.*

I had to hope that was true, that Torran hadn't noticed my bag of stolen supplies. Walking south to the settlement in the mountains would be difficult and dangerous — no way I would try it without first aid supplies for me and Malcolm.

I'd abandoned the bag under a table in the sickbay, and I had to hope no one found it and looked inside.

There wasn't any explanation or excuse for why I'd hoarded supplies for a trip, and if I got caught with them I knew that Torran's protection wouldn't be enough. Even if he backed me up, which I wasn't sure about. He'd protected me twice now, but if he realized I intended to run away, would that change?

I couldn't risk it. Despite how much I wanted to trust him, a mistake wouldn't just kill me. Malcolm's life was in my hands and no matter how good the alien warrior made me feel, I had to keep my focus. My brother's safety came first.

Torran can't have missed what I was up to, I thought, replaying the scene in my mind. I'd been right next to Torran when he woke, and if he hadn't seen or heard me grabbing the medicine, he *had* to have heard me drop the bag. I swallowed my fear, trying to build up my resolve. *That just means I have to leave quickly, before he decides to check what's in the bag or tells someone about it. I have to go tonight.*

The thought terrified me, but at least I wasn't putting it off any longer. I got my breathing under control and pulled myself together, going over what I laughably called a plan.

"Think, Lisa," I muttered. The planet was dangerous and neither Malcolm nor I were experienced hikers. Earth didn't have that much wilderness left to walk around in. As much as I hated to admit it, Carrington's hunting experience would have been handy for this trip.

But while I hoped the prytheen would just write off

the two of us, the more people involved in the escape the less likely they'd be to let us go. Putting that thought aside I went back to listing the gear Malcolm and I would need.

We'd need medical supplies, in case one of us got hurt. That I'd taken care of, assuming I could get that bag back. We'd need food for the trip. Fortunately the prytheen didn't pay much attention to the nutrient goop dispenser. They made a token effort to stop us stockpiling food but I'd managed to put aside a few days' worth. It might not be appetizing but it gave us a chance.

The big problem was weapons. Crashland wasn't a safe planet and the journey would be too dangerous without them. Maybe, if we still had our ultrasonic protection, we could do without. Arvid had seen to that, though.

I brushed my fingers across my wristband, feeling the furrows Arvid's knife had cut into two of its three speakers. The remaining one was enough for audible sounds — Henry could still bark — but not to broadcast the signal that kept native wildlife away.

Without rifles we stood no chance of making it to another settlement. Even with them, we didn't have much of a shot, but better to take it than wait here for Myrok to take his vengeance. Even if Torran kept me safe, Malcolm was vulnerable.

The prytheen *did* care about those, of course. They kept a careful watch on the armory, one of the prytheen watching it every hour of the day. I had a plan for getting past him but it wasn't safe and it had to be the last thing I did before we left. As soon as they discovered weapons were missing they'd be on high alert and that would blow everything.

Which meant that I needed to get my brother first, grab the weapons, and run. With luck we'd be too far away for the aliens to track down and they'd assume we'd died in the woods.

The family sleeping areas were all occupied by prytheen now, and the humans had been relegated to one of the storerooms. Packed as though we were just farming equipment. It made my blood boil, but I refused to let that anger distract me as I opened the door and slipped inside.

The small space was packed, sleeping bags laid out next to each other, and in the dark I had to step carefully to avoid treading on someone. Fortunately, Malcolm slept near the entrance and the dim light from my wristband's holo-emitter let me see well enough to find him quickly. I looked down at my brother's peaceful sleep and regretfully crouched over him to wake him up.

"Quiet," I hissed as Malcolm woke, my hand clamping over his mouth and muffling his gasp of fear. After a moment's half-asleep panic he subsided, calming and looking up at me with sleep filled eyes. He looked exhausted, and no wonder. The prytheen kept their human slaves hard at work every waking hour.

"We're getting out of here," I whispered into my brother's ear. His eyes widened and he nodded quickly, pulling himself out of his sleeping bag and grabbing his boots.

"How? Where are we going?" he whispered. At least he knew to keep his voice down, even if he was asking questions I didn't have a good answer to.

"South," I told him, leading him towards the door. "We'll sort out the details as we go. But we can't stay here. They'll kill us."

"This is because of me, isn't it?" He looked back, worried, as we slipped out of the storeroom and slid the door shut silently behind us. I guessed what he was thinking and winced guiltily. If we managed to escape, Gurral might decide to take it out on the other prisoners.

Nothing I could do about that, though. I took a little comfort in the fact that Gurral and his men couldn't afford to actually hurt their human slaves much in retaliation — they were already short on workers and couldn't afford to lose more. *They'll increase security, make it harder for others to escape,* I told myself, *but they won't punish anyone who stays.*

I almost believed it.

Malcolm repeated his question in an urgent whisper as I led him towards the armory. I turned, taking my brother by the shoulders and looking into his eyes.

"No, Malcolm, it's not your fault," I told him. "None of this is your fault. The prytheen are the ones to blame for everything they've done, not us — don't let them convince you that you deserve any of this."

It came out more fiercely than I'd intended, but it looked like it did the trick. A little shakily, Malcolm nodded and squared his shoulders. Good, I'd convinced him. Convincing myself was harder.

~

It wasn't really an armory, of course, but it was close enough. The secure storeroom around the corner from sickbay held all the guns not in use, as well as fuel stores and nanites. The point was to lock away equipment that might be dangerous rather than specifically to secure the rifles, but it served that purpose anyway.

Tinny laughter greeted us as we crept closer, and I peeked around the corner to see a prytheen guard leaning against the wall, watching something on a stolen holo-player. He had no reason to stay alert: unarmed, no human was a threat to a prytheen warrior, and all the weapons were locked up behind the door he guarded.

Time for my plan. My stupid, desperate plan. I ducked back, pulling Malcolm with me, and whispered in his ear.

"You stay here," I told him. "I'll be back in a second, just let me know if the guard moves."

"What if he comes this way?"

"Run and hide." Before he asked any more questions, I ducked into the sickbay. The door slid open silently and I stepped inside, glad of the low lighting. Torran lay on his bunk, chest rising and falling so slowly it was hard to see. Just looking at him made me feel safe, despite the fact that I was anything but. Even asleep his presence filled the room, and part of me wanted to stay there with him. Trust in him to protect me from the other prytheen.

But that wouldn't work. While my instincts insisted Torran would take my side against the other aliens, how could I believe that? He'd been part of the group that attacked us, after all. *Stick with the plan, Lisa. Get as far away from the aliens as you can.*

I moved as quietly as possible, circling the room to grab the bag I'd dropped earlier.

For a moment I considered stealing more supplies before leaving, but I stopped myself. No need to risk waking him and drawing his attention. He was the only one of the prytheen I'd rather not hurt.

Maybe I should drug him? I picked up a spray-hypo, turning it over and over in my hands, and shook my head. Getting that close to him risked waking him, and then what would I say to explain myself?

Better to avoid taking unnecessary chances. The ones I was planning to take were bad enough. I slipped the hypo into my pocket, slung the bag onto my back, and made my way back to Malcolm's side. He nodded at me, relaxing, and looked at me as if to say, 'now what?'

I swallowed nervously. This bit of the plan was crazy, but I had to chance it. I reached into my pocket for the spray-hypo I'd stolen.

It was full of the strongest sedative we had, and the

dose dialed up to maximum. I'd used it on Torran early on, keeping him under so he could heal. It *should* put a healthy prytheen down almost instantly. If only I'd had a chance to test it…

Malcolm tugged at my sleeve and I looked back at him. He shook his head firmly, face pale and eyes wide. Wanting to protect me as much as I wanted to defend him. I smiled sadly, wishing I had another choice.

We could still go back to our beds and forget about the escape. No one would know, we'd done nothing that couldn't be ignored. Not yet. But as soon as I stepped around the corner, we'd be committed. Escape or death would be our only options.

I felt the temptation. Just give up, go back to bed, and hope we'd survive. With an effort I shrugged it off. If we didn't go now, we wouldn't go at all. And sooner or later Myrok or one of the others would kill Malcolm.

No. Now, while I had the guts to do it. I shrugged off Malcolm's grip, drew myself up, and walked around the corner with all the confidence I could muster. I got three steps before the prytheen looked up at me, eyes narrowing suspiciously. Yeah, no chance that I'd have snuck up on him — even distracted by the comedy show, his alien senses were far too alert for me.

Instead I smiled and nodded, ignoring his growled inquiry and trusting that he'd underestimate me like every alien seemed to. Every one apart from the one I'd shot, at least, and he wasn't my enemy.

My heart pounded loud enough I thought the alien

would hear it, and the spray-hypo felt slippery in my sweaty fingers. The corridor felt so long, and though it only took a few steps to reach him it seemed like an eternity passed.

"What do you want?" he growled, voice deep and annoyed rather than suspicious. Another step, just smiling and nodding, trying to get in arm's reach. So close now, but not close enough.

His frown deepened, claws sliding out of his fingers as he drew himself up. I'd pushed this ruse as far as possible, and I needed one more step. Crap.

"Talk, human," he ordered, and I knew that this was it. My only chance. I tightened my grip on the hypo, took a deep breath. I'd have to risk a lunge and hope I reached him before he saw me coming.

And then, before I could act, Malcolm stepped around the corner behind me. "Sir! Message for you."

My blood turned to ice water as the prytheen's eyes snapped up to Malcolm. But something kicked in and I took advantage of his distraction without thinking about it. Stepping forward, I slapped the end of the hypo into the guard's arm. It activated with a hiss.

The next thing I knew I was bouncing off the wall. My jaw ached, the hypo went flying, and I tasted blood. Everything spun around me, and the alien loomed large over me, hand raised to strike. *Oh. He hit me.* It didn't seem important, somehow. I'd done what I'd planned to, and that was what mattered.

Above me, the alien paused. Growled, swayed, and slumped. His eyes unfocused and he muttered something under his breath before sliding down the wall to the floor. I watched, transfixed, as his eyes closed and he started to snore.

"Sis. Sis!" Malcolm shook me out of my shock, and I groaned as he helped me back to my feet. "Come on sis, we have to get out of here."

I nodded, stumbling past the fallen guard to the armory door. The ache in my jaw got worse as I moved it, but nothing felt broken. I just had to pray I didn't have a concussion or other lasting injuries, because there was no stopping now.

The door opened at my touch: it was just another storeroom as far as the pod's computer was concerned, accessible to any colonist above legal age. It logged who came in and out, but that would be obvious by the time anyone thought to check the computers.

I wasn't worried about what would happen in the morning. Not nearly as much as I worried about someone seeing the unconscious guard in the corridor before we were done gathering supplies.

"Grab a leg," I told my brother, taking hold of the guard's ankle. "Let's get him out of sight."

Dragging him into the storeroom wasn't easy, but I felt a little safer once he was out of sight. Turning, I looked at the gun racks. Batteries sat in their charging cradles, and beside them stood the rifles, stored neatly in a row. Two were missing, probably in prytheen hands. A locking bar held the remaining eight in place. That bar was all that stood in our way now.

I pressed my thumb to the lock's scanner. A beep

and a red light. Damn it. Wiping my sweaty hand on my pants I tried again. Another angry beep.

Malcolm's presence was all that kept me from swearing aloud. A third failed attempt would set off the alarm, and then we'd be dead. I took a deep breath and tried to think.

The answer was obvious. Of course the prytheen had changed the lock so it recognized their fingerprints rather than ours. I cursed under my breath and grabbed the guard by the wrist, heaving his arm up to touch the pad.

For a long, tense moment nothing happened. Then the light went green and the lock popped open. I offered up a silent prayer of thanks, fingers shaking as I reached for the nearest gun.

Behind me, Malcolm yelped and hit the floor with a heavy thump. A hand grabbed at me and I spun away, eyes wide as I looked at the guard. His hate-filled eyes glared at me as he dragged himself to his feet.

Fuck. I'd expected the drug to keep him out for hours, but it had only given me minutes.

"Kill you," he snarled in Galtrade, words slurred. "Kill you *slow*."

"Bite me," I retorted, fear washed out in a rush of adrenaline. My hands closed on a rifle, and I grabbed a battery pack from the charger.

Drugged or not, he was more than a match for me in hand to hand. With a rifle, though, the odds changed.

I'd shot one prytheen, I could shoot another. I told

myself that as I fumbled to load the battery into the weapon, the alien staggering towards me as Malcolm writhed on the floor.

I almost made it. The battery clicked home and the laser hummed to life. But his reflexes were too fast, and before I could bring the barrel around to point at him, he knocked it aside.

With a crack, the laser went off. The flash of light was blinding in the dark room, and even worse for the prytheen with his sensitive eyes. He howled in pain, flinching back and yanking the weapon from my hands.

My one chance and I'd blown it.

8

TORRAN

*L*isa was no stealthier the second time she snuck into the sickbay, and I woke immediately. I smelled her fear, heard it in the quick pulse of her blood, felt it like a pressure against my heart. This time I stayed motionless, resolving to see what she planned before interfering. She didn't trust me enough to tell me.

Once she left the room, I stood carefully and took stock of my condition. My wound ached but my strength returned, and I stretched this way and that. Yes, I could fight if need be. Hopefully that wouldn't be necessary, and whatever trouble she'd gotten herself into would not require violence to solve.

But she was my khara. If I had to kill to protect her, to save her, I would. My body burned for her and I would not allow anyone to harm a single hair on her beautiful head.

I moved to the door, ready at last to follow her. As it slid open, a laser shot echoed in the corridor.

I'd never moved so fast. Dashing around the corner, I saw Rarric standing in the door to the armory. One of Gurral's men, not one I knew well. His fury was plain from the tension in his muscles and a scorch mark showed where a laser blast had struck the floor beside him.

He held a laser rifle one handed, aiming it into the room. And my instincts told me who he threatened. White hot rage flashed through me and I charged without a thought.

Rarric spun at the sound of my approach, pulling the rifle up towards me. Not fast enough — I was too close, and surprise slowed his reactions. Diving forward, I slammed into him, sending the rifle flying as we tumbled to the floor in a struggling mess of limbs.

His claws raked my back and I snarled in pain, clawing his side in turn. Both of us were bloody as we parted, rolling to our feet and facing off in the small space.

"Traitor," he spat at me, drawing a knife. "I'll gut you and the humans."

I didn't waste words on threats. We were beyond posturing now, and one of us had to die here. If Rarric lived, Lisa would die — and that I wouldn't allow.

Instead of going for my own blades, I rushed in again, feinting left before ducking right. His knife slashed through where he thought I'd be, and before he got it back between us, I slashed his arm with my claws. The blade went flying, but his counter-punch smashed into my ribs and I winced at the impact.

Have to win this quick, before anyone hears the struggle, I thought, diving in and ignoring the punishing blows he landed as I got close. A sweep to my legs took me off balance, but I turned the fall into a tackle and we tumbled over and over.

This time I didn't let him separate us. Close in, we tore at each other, and I bit back my pain. No time for that, not now.

He grabbed another knife from his belt, and I grabbed his wrist. Pinning him, just for a moment. Just long enough to draw my own knife and open his throat. Blood sprayed and Rarric spasmed under me. His eyes widened with shock before dimming as the life left them.

I waited until I was sure before letting go, sitting up with a pained growl. New injuries to add to the old. Great. At least none of them were deep, but they stung like hell.

Inside the room, the humans huddled against the far wall. Lisa struggled to load another rifle while her brother stared in wide-eyed shock at the doorway.

"You're safe now," I said. An exaggeration, a huge one, but I had to say something.

Lisa's laser rifle wavered as she trained it on me and I remembered our first meeting. The still-healing wound she'd left in me burned, and my fresh injuries stung as I slowly, carefully, stepped forward.

I could have disarmed her easily. At this range the

rifle was a poor choice of weapon, too unwieldy and heavy in her hands. One quick grab and I'd have it.

But I didn't want to leave her defenseless, and this time she wouldn't shoot. Another step and the barrel brushed against me, and then she lowered it carefully.

"You are safe," I repeated. "I will not let anyone hurt you while I have breath in my body."

Tears welled in her eyes and she sobbed, flinging herself at me. I caught her, ignoring the pain where her arms squeezed my injured torso. A small price to pay to hold my khara, to comfort her in her shock and dismay.

"I thought we were going to die," she sobbed. I barely made out the words through her tears. "Oh god, they're going to kill us."

"They will not," I promised, hoping that I could keep that oath. "I will slay anyone who tries to hurt you, my khara. You and your brother are safe."

Lisa pulled back, tear-stained face looking up at me. She wasn't fooled, of course. She knew as well as I did that there would be no forgiveness for killing a member of Gurral's clan. But still she managed a weak smile.

"You're a pretty good liar," she said, squeezing me. "But we're well and truly fucked, aren't we?"

I didn't know how to respond to that. Anyone else who called me a liar would face me in a duel, but not my khara. And she wasn't *wrong:* I'd tell whatever lies needed to keep her safe.

Lisa wiped her sleeve across her face, hands trembling gently. Took a deep breath and looked down at Rarric's corpse. Her face paled again at the sight, looking as though she was about to be sick. I felt it too, my stomach turning — not at the sight of death but at the thought of my khara joining him.

I would fight to defend her against any odds but against Gurral and all his men I would lose. The only chance she had was to get far away while I bought her time with my life.

It would be a death worthy of a warrior, at least. I tried to take comfort in that.

9

LISA

Looking down at the bloody corpse of the prytheen warrior, I clenched my jaw and tried to control my nausea. If Torran hadn't appeared at exactly the right moment, it would be me and Malcolm lying dead on the floor.

The store room started to spin around me and I grabbed hold of Torran to steady myself. *I can't faint, not now. I have to be strong enough to get Malcolm out of here.*

Torran's strong body, the warmth of his skin, the strong male scent of him, all of that gave me the strength I needed. I clung to him like a drowning sailor to a life raft. His powerful arms closed around me, holding me with careful strength, and I felt safe for the first time since the crash.

That's insane, I thought as I held on tight. *I'm standing over a dead body, the other aliens will kill me and Malcolm and Torran for this, and* now *I feel safe?*

Reason had nothing to do with it, though. Torran held me tight and safe and secure, and I buried my face against his chest and stifled a sob.

If only I could stay there forever. But I had work to do if we were going to survive this.

"You must go," he growled, his deep voice vibrating through me. "Quickly, before anyone discovers what has happened."

"*We* have to go," I said, pushing my emotions down into a tight ball in my chest. Later, when I had time, I could have a panic attack. Right now I had to think. "If you stay, they'll kill you."

"That is true," he said as though that didn't matter at all. "But I will slow them down while you and your brother escape. Go, Lisa. Now."

I lifted my head from his chest to look up at him, biting my lip. "No. I won't leave you behind to die for me."

His frustrated growl filled the small room and he stepped back to look down at me. "Lisa, when Gurral finds out about this he will be furious. You cannot be here when that happens: if you are, he will certainly kill you. Probably the other humans too."

I blinked at that, taken by surprise. It took a moment to sink in, and I felt a surge of fear that threatened to overwhelm me. "He can't, he needs them to do the work."

"He's already planning on capturing more human slaves," Torran said, shaking his head. "And he'll want to make an example of what happens when someone escapes or hurts one of the prytheen. You must leave before he finds out about this."

I wanted to doubt him, to say that he was wrong and even Gurral wouldn't be so brutal. Unfortunately I couldn't. The sheer unwavering certainty in his eyes, the edge in his voice, the urgency… Torran believed this with all his heart. I had to trust him.

Which only made things worse.

"I can't leave the others to die," I protested, pacing up and down the tiny room. Too much nervous energy, I had to let it out somehow. "It's my fault they'll be killed."

"No!" Torran interrupted, quiet but sharp. "No, Lisa, it's Gurral's responsibility and no one else's. You aren't to blame for what he does."

Kind words, but I didn't believe them. My actions would get the others killed if I ran now, and I couldn't let that happen.

"I'll take them with me." The words were out of my mouth before I'd thought about them.

Torran let out a sound half way between a groan and a desperate laugh. "A group that size will be hunted down in hours at best. You and Malcolm stand a chance if you cover your tracks and I keep Gurral from following you too quickly. Nine humans fleeing on foot? You'd be lucky to live till dawn."

I opened my mouth to argue, then shut it again with a snap. He was right — the Dietrich's had no woodcraft skills, and while Carrington and his sons were good hunters, I doubted they'd stay ahead of the prytheen for long.

That didn't mean they deserved to die, but how could we save them all?

"The rover," Malcolm exclaimed. Torran and I both looked at him and he blushed, shrinking away from the alien. My brother didn't feel as safe in Torran's presence as I did.

But he didn't let that stop him. "We assemble the rover. It can carry us all easy, and it's a lot faster than walking."

Torran frowned, looking back at me with a question in his eyes. I nodded thoughtfully, afraid to hope. Maybe Malcolm's idea would work — and if it did, we could save Torran too. He wouldn't have to stay behind to protect us.

"Every colony pod has a hover vehicle," I explained. "Ours is still in storage, we'd need to put it together, but once we have it, it'd be so much faster than walking. We can all get away in that, Gurral won't be able to catch up."

Torran frowned and I could see a thousand objections in his eyes. Not without reason — the forest was bad terrain for a vehicle and assembling it would take time we might not have. I didn't wait for him to say it out loud, pushing ahead and trying to think of ways around the problems.

"We'll need help to get it assembled fast," I started, ticking off points on my fingers. "That means getting Maria to help, she's the best engineer with us. And it'll take time so we need to keep Gurral and his men from finding out about *this*."

My gesture took in the bloody mess of the body on the floor. I didn't want to look at it, but we had to do something. Just ignoring it wasn't an option.

Torran shook his head. "As soon as one of them comes down here they'll smell the blood. No matter where we hide the body, they'll track it down in minutes."

I frowned, looked around the storeroom, an idea starting to form in my mind. I pulled packs of nanites from the shelves, stuffed as many as possible into a bag.

"Leave that to me," I said, hoping my half-formed plan would work. "As long as you can get the body out to the fields, I think I can deal with it."

His lips twitched, and he looked at me. "Even if you can hide the body, that will only buy you a day, two at best. But very well, I shall get him outside. If you're sure you want to take this risk?"

"Yes," I said, relief flooding through me. It was a terrible plan, full of things that could go wrong, but if it worked it might just save us all. Even Torran, which mattered more than I thought it would. "Yes, Torran, I do. Thank you."

He nodded, not looking convinced. "Fine. I will do my best to cover for you. Get the other humans ready to go as quickly as possible, because you will not have long. Probably no more than a day."

I nodded quickly and threw my arms around him, hugging him tight. "Thank you!"

I wanted to kiss him. Despite his doubts he was willing to try things my way, and that gave us all a chance. Unless I was wrong, of course, in which case I might get us all killed. I tried not to think about that as I hauled down the buckets of powerful cleaning gear from the shelves.

10

TORRAN

Whatever Lisa's plan was, I had to hope it was worth the work I put into it. We got to work quickly, Lisa and her brother hauling out the foul-smelling chemicals that humans used to clean and starting to scrub the decking as I pulled down a tarp and wrapped the corpse in it. I taped it shut carefully to make certain no blood would leak: leaving a trail outside would doom us all.

We couldn't afford to leave any trace of the fight outside the armory, and that meant being thorough as well as fast.

Once he was ready to transport, I looked around. The humans had done good work on the bloody mess the fight had left, and I couldn't see any sign of it. Smell was another matter, though. Even through the harsh chemical scent of the cleaning products the bitter copper tang of blood was obvious.

"Go over it again," I growled. The humans looked up, surprised. "I can still tell there was a fight here."

Lisa chewed on her lip, looking at the tarp-wrapped bundle. "We've got to get rid of that first. There's no point in hiding the blood if Gurral sees the body."

I frowned but nodded.

"Fine. We'll deal with it; your brother can keep cleaning." The human boy looked almost relieved not to have to deal with a corpse and nodded quickly. Lisa didn't look happy to leave him behind, but nodded, recognizing the necessity. She grabbed her bag and I lifted the corpse, cursing Rarric for his weight.

No one watched the exit, thank the ancestors. The prytheen outside gathered around a fire far from the pod, and I heard laughter and jokes. The camaraderie of a clan forming, the scent of cooking meat, the sounds of companionship. No one paid any attention to the pod itself, giving us a chance to sneak out.

As quietly as possible, we lowered ourselves to the ground and ducked out of sight behind the pod. I put down the body and listened for any sign they'd noticed us.

Nothing. The party went on unchanged.

"Now what?" I asked. Left here the body might go unseen until the morning, but as decay set in nothing would hide its smell.

Lisa stared at the corpse long enough that I began to worry. Did my khara really have a plan? But then she set down her bag and took out the packages she'd picked from the storeroom's shelves.

Tearing them open one by one, she scattered a fine silvery powder over Rarric's remains. Once he was thoroughly covered in the stuff she stepped back and took my hand.

"Do you, um, have something you say for the dead?" she asked, frowning. "This is as close to a funeral as he'll get."

I sighed and nodded. The words should be spoken by an Alpha-Captain or someone close to him, but that was impossible. I'd have to do, and if I wasn't enough, well, he shouldn't have gotten himself killed attacking my khara.

"Find peace in your next life, Rarric," I told him. "Go tell the ancestors you fell in honorable battle."

That might not be strictly true, but I wouldn't grudge him the formal words of burial. It cost me nothing, and if it gave his spirit peace then that hurt no one.

Turning to my khara, I nodded to her. She hit a button on her wristband, conjuring her strange hologram interface. The translucent bundle of fluff looked from her to the bundled-up corpse as Lisa issued instructions. Quick, muttered words and fast gestures changed settings on the interface and the virtual mammal stalked around the dead prytheen. Beneath its paws, the silver dust sparkled and hissed, nanites activating and going to work. The corpse began to dissolve as I watched, steaming as it sank in on itself.

Soon there was nothing recognizable left of him,

only a pile of organic matter that would serve as fertilizer for new life.

"That was all the nanites we had left," Lisa said absently. "No more tree stumps getting cleared that way."

"Let us hope you aren't here long enough to need any," I said, guiding her away with a hand on her shoulder. Tired and upset, she didn't need to see the results of her handiwork on the dead.

"We'd better get you back to your brother," I said, leading her towards the open door. Now that the body was gone the weight on my shoulders felt lighter, though I knew that was an illusion. Rarric would be missed soon, at morning if not before, and once Gurral realized he was dead things would go very badly very quickly.

Back in the pod we found Malcolm still desperately scrubbing away at the hall. The overpowering chemical smell filled the corridor and I almost gagged on it. I could still detect a hint of blood under the chemical odor despite all his work, and I snarled in frustration. We'd simply have to risk it. I knew to look for it — perhaps others who didn't would miss the scent.

"Enough," I told him. "You two had better get going."

"Not until I've dressed those wounds," Lisa said firmly, ducking into the sickbay and returning with a can of spray bandages. I looked down and cursed. Of course I could smell blood, Rarric had opened a dozen cuts in my skin.

The icy sensation of the spray was uncomfortable but soon over. Once she'd finished, Lisa gave me a hug and kissed my injuries before hurrying away to her fellows.

I sighed, leaning against the wall where Rarric had stood watch, waiting for his relief to arrive. Frustration filled my bones — I'd rather have been moving, doing something, but I needed to buy time for Lisa and her desperate plan to save us all.

We have one chance in a thousand, no more, I thought. But if my khara wanted to take that gamble I would back her play with all my skill and strength. I'd just have to pray that it was enough.

11

LISA

Malcolm and I returned to the human barracks as quietly as we'd left. The others still slept, blissfully unaware of the danger we were all in. It felt like a shame to wake them but what choice did we have? They needed to know, deserved to know.

Ignorance might be bliss, but in this case it was also a death sentence.

Moving quickly around the room, we quietly woke each of the other humans. They gathered around us, tired and confused and annoyed, until we were at the center of a grumbling semicircle. The ghostly light of our holograms illuminated the room, lending the meeting a conspiratorial air.

"What the devil do you want with us at this hour," Mr. Carrington said, consulting his wristband hologram to see the time. "We should be asleep, there's a lot of work to do tomorrow."

"More than you realize," I said. "We're going to escape."

A mutter ran around the room and I tried to read the faces of my fellow prisoners. Springing this on them all at once was a huge risk, but there wasn't time to do it differently.

Maria Dietrich looked shocked but nodded decisively, which took a huge weight off my chest. Her skill as an engineer would be vital to getting the rover ready in time. Alex Dietrich looked less certain, but I knew he'd stick with his wife. Good.

The Carringtons were another story. The three boys looked excited more than anything else, eyes shining at the idea of an adventure. Better than nothing, but it didn't look like we could trust them to be discreet about it. *At least the secret only has to last one day.*

Mr. Carrington's face was like thunder, though. A deep red flush spread over his cheeks and his eyes narrowed as he leaned forward to glare at me. "Don't be stupid, child. Your foolishness will get us all killed."

"If we stay here, we'll all die anyway," I countered, keeping myself from flinching by sheer stubbornness. I'd seen someone die tonight; Carrington was a lot less frightening than that. "We have to go, and we have to go now. I need your help to make it happen."

He snorted and shook his head, unimpressed. "Young lady, I know that running off into the forest sounds like an exciting adventure. But we'd be escaping into the deadly terrain of an unknown world without a plan or sufficient supplies. If the prytheen don't hunt us down, we'll die on the march."

"Not if we take the rover," Malcolm interrupted excitedly. "We'll be too fast for them to catch us and safe from the wildlife. And we'll have Torran to scout a path for us."

Carrington snorted at that, not taking his eyes off me. "Hardly safe, boy. The terrain around here is no friend to vehicles, even if we can get it set up. No, the risk is far too high. We're safe here, secure and well fed. We stay."

For a moment I gaped at him. Safer as slaves? Was he really content with a life of drudgery, farming for the prytheen?

I couldn't believe it, but he seemed sincere. When I'd come up with this plan, I'd assumed he'd try to take over, but I'd never imagined he'd object to the escape itself. And if he meant it, would he rat the rest of us out? That would be the end of us all. Looking him in the eyes, all I could see was barely suppressed anger.

"I'm going," I said simply, turning from him to look at the rest of the humans. In the dim lighting it was hard to read their expressions but I pressed on. "Along with anyone who wants to risk coming with me. Freedom is worth taking a chance for, right?"

"Yes." Alex Dietrich surprised me by being the first to speak up. "We are with you."

His wife squeezed his hand and I breathed a little easier. At least someone listened to reason.

The Carrington boys looked at their father for leadership, and I prayed that he'd see sense. But he shook his head firmly.

"The rest of you may go to your deaths," he said, contempt showing in his voice. "I am not so foolish and neither are my sons. We will stay: the prytheen are wise enough not to punish those who remain loyal when the rest of you flee to your doom."

It was hard to tell in the low light but I didn't think his sons agreed with his argument. Still, none of them argued. David, the oldest, looked particularly mutinous, but he stayed silent and deferred to his father.

What the hell do I do about that? I asked myself. *Let him sentence his family to slavery out of fear?*

I sighed. It was their choice, and we couldn't force them. All of them were adults, and if they were going to listen to their father's bad advice I couldn't force them to come.

"You're all welcome to join us," I said. "If you want to stay, though, it's up to you."

Carrington snorted and shook his head. "We will not commit suicide for your harebrained plans, girl. No, my boys and I will stay here and show the prytheen that *some* humans can be trusted."

I hoped he couldn't read the disgust in my expression. His cowardice would endanger us all but there wasn't anything I could do about that. As long as he didn't betray the rest of us, I'd have to accept it.

"We can trust you too, right?" I asked. "You have to promise us you won't tell Gurral or his men about our plan."

Carrington's nose wrinkled as though he'd smelled something nasty, but he nodded, glancing at his boys. They were on the verge of mutiny and even he could see that — staying behind was one thing, turning on his fellow humans was another.

"Of course I won't," he said. "You can make your own damned fool mistakes. We won't say a word about your little plan."

And as little as I thought of him, he'd never struck me as a liar. A lot of other things, yes, but not that. I breathed a bit easier and hoped he and his family would survive his error.

"Thank you," I said as sincerely as I could before turning to the others. "We'll all need to cover for Maria while she puts together the rover tomorrow, so it'll be hard work. With luck we'll get on the road tomorrow night and head for the valley settlement."

"One problem," Alex said, scratching his head. "Food. We can steal a little, certainly, but the matter processor doesn't make that much at once and the other rations are long gone."

"We can go hungry a day or two," Malcolm said, but Alex didn't look convinced. Neither was I. We were already hungry and low on energy.

"A day or two is fine," Alex said, "but what if it takes longer than that? No one knows the route we're taking, what if it we need a week to reach help?"

Maria laughed. It wasn't a particularly mirthful sound. "There's an obvious answer, Alex. We've already traveled for months without eating to reach this planet.

All we have to do is put ourselves in the stasis tubes again and haul those."

The look Alex gave his wife wasn't entirely happy, but he sighed. "Yes. I suppose that will work. Say two drivers taking turns, the rest of us in stasis, that will let us stretch the food supplies a lot further. Fine. Tomorrow we get on the road."

Everyone nodded, and I hoped it would be that easy. For a start, there wasn't an actual road, and we were gambling that the crash hadn't damaged any vital parts of the rover. Then there was the long, dangerous drive to the mountains.

But it didn't matter. Taking the risk was better than staying here, whatever Carrington thought.

12

TORRAN

*O*nce Lisa and her brother were away, I sighed with relief and turned to tidying the storeroom. It might be clean, but it also had to be neat — no one who visited it could suspect that there had been a fight here.

The cleaning supplies went back on the shelves, and I spaced them out a little hoping that no one would notice the missing nanite packages. I put the rifles back in place then paused, thinking. It would be easier to cross the uncharted forest if I had a rifle to hunt with, and it might help with another problem too.

Rarric's absence would be missed, and I needed an excuse for his disappearance. Perhaps I could solve two problems at once. Taking one rifle and power pack, I hid them in the sickbay and then replaced the rest on their racks, relocking the bar that secured them in place. That done, I took up position outside the room. I didn't have to wait long before I heard someone approach.

Tarva turned the corner and stopped in surprise. "Torran? What are you doing here? I'm supposed to relieve Rarric."

I hid my relief behind a smile. Tarva knew and trusted me more than Gurral's people did, which made it easier to fool her. I felt a pang of guilt at that and ruthlessly suppressed it.

Lying was the least of the things I'd do to protect my khara.

"Eh, I felt cooped up stuck in the sickbay all the time," I told her. "I'm fit enough to guard a door, and Rarric was glad to get away early."

She snorted. "Couldn't you have waited for my shift to take over?"

I shook my head, trying to look amused. "Sorry I didn't consult the schedule, Tarva. But I'll stand your watch too, if you like. You'll owe me one, though."

Tarva laughed and nodded. "Fine, I'll add that to what I owe you already, but it's just a drop in a tankful. I still have to repay you for getting us here in one piece — Dessus, Arvid, and me, we'd have starved in the wilderness without your help. Or been eaten by the wildlife."

I tried to hide my wince. Tarva might remember that as a favor I'd done her, but if I hadn't saved them Lisa wouldn't be in danger now. On the other hand, I would never have met Lisa. *The past is behind me, leave it there. Look to the future.*

"Get some rest or do some hunting," I said. "And you can pay me back with some fresh meat. It's been too long since I've been able to hunt for myself."

"Aye, well, if you will let a human shoot you, that's what you get," she said with a grin and a wave as she turned away. "Be more careful in future, okay? We all need friends here."

I nodded and waved back, letting her turn the corner before letting out a quiet sigh of relief. Not every survivor of the Silver Band was my enemy. Or at least, not yet. How would she feel once I'd freed the humans? We might still end up being mortal enemies.

But at least I didn't have to fight her now. It was a strange night where that counted as a positive.

The wait for morning took forever and every second I listened for the sounds of alarm. Instead, Myrok came to relieve me at dawn, as the humans filed out to work the fields. I met Lisa's eye as she passed and she gave me a subtle nod. Good. Neither of us had failed the first hurdle.

Now I just had to hope that the rest of this terrible plan went as smoothly. I didn't fully believe it would work, but I would do my best for Lisa's sake. If nothing else good came of it, we'd have some time together. Catching her by the arm, I led her into the shadow of the pod, out of sight.

"Careful, you'll give us away," she protested, looking around to see if anyone had spotted us. I laughed.

"You are my khara, my mate," I said. "No one will question me taking you somewhere alone, little one."

"I don't even know what that *means*," she protested, her cheeks flushing at the implication. "That's not a Galtrade word."

"Khara?" I smiled at her, watching the shiver of desire that shot through her as a result. "It means you are everything to me. That you are the other part of my soul. The female fate has chosen me for, the one I would die to protect. My mate, my heart, my life."

She blushed and bit her lip, and I couldn't stop my body responding to her. She was too desirable for words, and I ached to take her then and there. To show her the pleasure I could give my mate and know her body as I should.

There is no time, I told myself, resisting the urge. Lisa's breath caught as she saw my reaction and her hand brushed my arm sending a wave of desire through me. Nearly enough to force me to action. I pulled back, breathing heavily and struggling to keep my mind on target. Lisa stepped away too, and for a moment we were silent, struggling with our urges.

"Is everything prepared for our escape?" I asked, trying to focus on the important thing: getting Lisa to safety.

For a moment it looked like she didn't understand, then she nodded. "Yes. I mean, almost. The Carringtons won't come."

The name meant nothing to me, but that didn't matter. Any of the humans remaining behind was bad news for them, but as long as they didn't betray Lisa it was their decision to make.

"They are free to make their own mistakes," I said. "As long as you and Malcolm get away, I shall be content."

Lisa nodded. "You're right, but I don't like leaving them behind to die."

"Perhaps they can convince Gurral of their loyalty," I suggested. It was a dubious possibility, but I wished them luck. He might listen.

In the end it didn't matter. Freedom included the freedom to make bad choices — they had made theirs.

Some would say my own decision to help Lisa escape was as foolish. Looking down at her, the soft and fragile human fate had paired me with, I knew that they were wrong. Lisa's freedom and happiness meant more to me than my own life.

She looked back at me, and the spark in her eyes was too much to resist. Her need echoed my own, and I could no longer fight the mating urge in my soul.

No. That wasn't true. I could have fought it — but I did not wish to.

I leaned in over her, pressing her back against the curved wall of the colony pod. Her face heated, a flush spreading across her cheeks, and her hands rose to press against my chest.

The feel of her hands made me growl, and she bit her lip again. A delightful sight that made me harden, my body aching for hers. Had she pushed me away I would have stepped back, but her resistance melted like ice in the heat of her desire.

"Torran," she breathed my name and it was the

sweetest poetry I had ever heard. I growled in response, enjoying the delighted shiver that ran through my khara's body as I bent for a kiss.

And then I heard the footsteps behind me. With a frustrated snarl, I spun to face a prytheen warrior as he came into view. Lisa shrank back behind me as the warrior spoke.

"Torran," he said. "Gurral is looking for you."

The warrior looked at us with a smirk and my hands tensed to rip and tear. Frustrated anger nearly boiled over, might have if Lisa hadn't taken my hand. Her touch reminded me of the need for patience.

"I must go," I said, turning back to Lisa and squeezing her hand before letting go. "I'll return as soon as I can."

Before she could respond, I turned away. Part of me feared that this would be the last time I'd see her, that our poorly thought out plan would fall apart before we were reunited. Perhaps I was going to my death.

If so, I would go with my head held high, and I'd die fighting. I promised myself that much.

The prytheen warrior led me inside, into the heart of the colony pod. Into the chambers that had been the humans' living quarters before we'd seized control and relegated them to the storage areas, as though they were merely equipment.

I wasn't impressed by the use the warriors were putting the place to. They'd converted the space into barracks by simply piling soft furnishings on the floor and nesting, and for the first time I felt grateful for the uncomfortable bed I'd been confined to in the sickbay. It had been too small, too hard, but it was a *bed*, not a pile of cloth.

Even in the wilderness outside I'd have made myself more comfortable than they had here. With an effort I hid my contempt at the laziness of the warriors and followed my guide through a curtained doorway into Gurral's lair.

The change was immediate and obvious. Gurral had kept enough space to set himself up with a comfortable bed in one corner, and a desk to work at opposite it. A low table held food, bread and fresh-cooked meat, ready for when he wanted it. And behind the desk, mounted on the wall, two laser rifles hung. A display of power and a weapon should anyone try to take his position.

Gurral himself sat behind the desk, flicking through holographic records while a radio hissed reports at him. Some in prytheen, some in a human language, and some in Galtrade. Too much to take in all at once, the chatter of the planet's new colonies surrounded us.

He didn't acknowledge me, and I refused to give him the pleasure of drawing his attention. Time stretched out as he sketched on a map, adjusting details in the hologram that floated above his desk until at last, finished with his current task, he looked up at me.

"You're on your feet at last, Torran," he said with a sly smile that didn't reach his eyes. "A quick recovery from yesterday."

"The promise of a hunt did a lot to speed things up,"

I said, trying to sound eager. "Something better to look forward to than overseeing a farm."

He laughed, slapping the desk. "Yes, I should have known that would motivate you. A scout needs to be active, not sit around watching the humans work."

Tension filled the air, and his forced humor didn't help. I stepped closer, trying to judge the situation. If he knew about Rarric's death we'd be having a very different conversation, but *something* was wrong.

"You didn't call me up here to congratulate me on my recovery," I said, glancing at the map and then at him. Since I was here anyway, I might as well use the opportunity to learn something. "You've got a plan in mind. An attack?"

Gurral nodded, brushing his hand through the hologram. The image rippled around his fingers and he traced a line south, through the forests to an area outlined in red. The map had few details, nothing I'd rely on, but the crimson area was nestled in a valley between the mountains.

"Here," he said with a predatory smile. "Humans have gathered in good farmland, set themselves up. They've got a strong position, one they do not wish to leave for the long trip to the *Wandering Star*."

"Then why are you here, and not there? Why settle for conquering this tiny community?"

"You are a clever man, Torran. You tell me."

I looked at the crude map, considering. The position of the mountains would be accurate, but the rest was guesswork and makeshift interpretation of the humans' radio signals. If it was anything like accurate, though, that valley would be easy to protect. A small fortification at the entrance and they'd be able to keep out the poorly armed warriors of Gurral's band.

"You need to find a way to sneak up on their defenses."

Gurral grinned, baring sharp teeth and nodding. "I've only a handful of warriors, and our blasters do not work. Even with the weapons we've gathered here, we are poorly equipped — there are only enough rifles for half of us, and they are puny lasers. Humans may be weak, but any losses they inflicted would be too many.

"Give me working blasters and I'd conquer the valley in a day. With what we have…"

I nodded. It would only take a few armed humans to control the valley's entrance and from cover they'd be a serious threat. But if Gurral got past them, into the heart of the valley… well, perhaps he overestimated his ability to conquer. Humans weren't the weaklings we'd thought when we'd come to this planet, after all. Even if he failed to rule them, though, the slaughter he'd unleash would be unfathomable.

Steep, rocky cliffs marked either side of the valley. Tough terrain, especially with hostile wildlife to contend with and possibly human patrols to watch for. The valley mouth made for a better way in, but an alert guard would have plenty of time to spot attackers coming.

The biggest difficulty would be reaching the valley without alerting the humans. Rough terrain, unexplored forest and hills filled with potential dangers lay between the two human enclaves. Crossing it, even with a small band of warriors, was an invitation to disaster. Unless someone with my experience scouted the way for them and got them to their destination both safely and quietly.

It wouldn't be easy, but this was exactly the work that Terasi had gathered her clan for. Part of me longed for the challenge.

I could do it, get them close and find a way past the defenses. But I would not. I'd seen the conditions Gurral thought fit for humans, and the Code of the Silver Band taught us to be better than that.

Even if not for the Code, Lisa's people deserved better.

"Won't Auric and his warriors object?" I asked, gauging the situation. "They've got the *Wandering Star* now, don't they?"

"Pah. Cowards who refuse to seize control from the human captain? I don't fear them. Oh, they'd resist if we attacked them directly, but I doubt they'll send their fighters halfway around the planet to strike at us once we're the ones in a defensible position. Besides, they have dangers closer to home to deal with."

Was that true? I didn't know, but it also didn't matter. Whether Auric sent aid to these humans or not, it would be too late to stop the conquest.

One more reason to get out of here before I help Gurral commit an atrocity, I told myself. *Not that I need one: saving Lisa is reason enough on its own.*

I put those thoughts aside and focused on the map, memorizing it. A rough sketch of the terrain we'd be crossing was better than nothing. If I delivered Lisa and her companions to the valley they'd be safe, or as close to it as anyone on Crashland was.

"I can get you in there," I told Gurral, full of confidence. "It won't be quick or easy though."

"There is no rush," he promised. "Specialist work takes time, I understand that. Remember that there's a limit, though. The humans' crops grow fast, and the hunting is good, but we can't wait around here forever."

I met his gaze, weighing his words. I knew what 'no rush' meant from a leader like this — he'd expect results soon, no matter what he said. And I couldn't afford for Gurral to realize I had doubts about his plan, so I nodded.

"All I need is a few days to prepare," I said. "Then I'll find your path. I need to be sure I'm fit for the journey, and to get used to the equipment I have available."

The thought of it was exhilarating, even if it was a lie. The chance to test myself against this planet, to see what I could do alone with no tool more advanced than a laser rifle. My fingers itched for it, for the taste and smell and feel of a new world to conquer. But I wouldn't be alone.

Instead, I'd travel with the humans. Take them to safety. As great a challenge as it would be to attack the valley, it would be an even greater challenge to save Lisa and her people.

I met Gurral's suspicious gaze and bared my teeth, letting him see my hunger for conquest. He looked deep, weighing me and my commitment, and then nodded. My eagerness to go fitted with his design.

Paranoid though he was, he had no reason to suspect what I actually planned to do. My plan to steal away his human slaves was too crazy for him to even consider.

13

LISA

The day passed at an excruciating crawl as we all tried to act normal. It wasn't easy, especially since none of us had gotten enough sleep, and we had to rely on the fact that the prytheen barely paid us any attention. The one advantage of being thought inferior: they didn't conceive of us as a threat, not now they'd conquered us.

Maria slipped away into pod's workshop halfway through the morning, leaving the rest of us short-handed. It hardly mattered. As long as we looked busy the prytheen were unlikely to count us — all they watched for was slacking off or escape attempts.

As long as the rest of us took up the slack, they wouldn't notice a missing slave. At least, I hoped they wouldn't — if they did it would be the end of our stupid little escape attempt.

It meant a hard day's work for me after a night without sleep, but I wasn't the only one working hard.

Malcolm, bless him, threw himself into the work, and Alex did too. Even the Carrington boys worked extra hard, and they weren't even coming on the escape.

Only their father seemed to lack enthusiasm, and he'd never been one for working. Encouraging the rest of us, yes, or at least shouting at us when he thought we were slacking off — but actual hard work didn't seem to be in his repertoire.

It seemed like a waste of effort to put this much work into fields we'd hopefully never see again, but there was no helping that. With the Carringtons remaining behind we might as well help them... and there was always the chance that our escape failed. Probably that would mean death, but if not, at least there'd be crops to come back to.

Anyway, working hard gave me something to focus on aside from my worries, for which I was grateful. The bright sun passed overhead as I struggled with the branches of fallen trees, clearing space with Malcolm's help. But eventually my arms gave up, my fatigue catching up with me.

"I'll check on Maria, see if I can help her with the rover," I told my brother, wiping sweat from my brow. "I can't lift any more."

He nodded, shooting a nervous glance at the watching prytheen. "Okay, sis. Take care *they* don't see you."

I nodded, giving him a quick hug. "Keep an eye on Carrington," I whispered before we parted. "I don't quite trust him."

His eyes went wide and he nodded wordlessly. I hid a smile. I didn't trust Carrington, that much was true, but more importantly this gave Malcolm something to focus on aside from the danger we were in. While his attention was on Carrington, he wouldn't be staring at the prytheen.

It was near enough our unofficial lunchtime that I had a ready-made excuse for leaving the field. I made my way into the pod with as much confidence as I could muster. Anyone watching should see a human on her way to get her meager rations, not someone sneaking off.

But instead of heading to the mess and the food dispenser, I slipped into the engineering bay. Maria had the rover half-assembled already, and she spun around with a guilty look on her face when I stepped inside.

"Don't sneak up on me like that," she said, fingers tight on a wrench and hand shaking. "I almost panicked and attacked you."

"Sorry," I said, wondering if the wrench would even give one of the prytheen pause. For all their faults, every one of them was a formidable enemy and without a gun I doubted any of us could face one in a fight.

Better not to find out. Once the rover was ready, we'd put miles between us and the prytheen. All except Torran, and he was different.

Still frightening, but different. My fear of him blurred into excitement and thinking of him chasing me down made me tingle and blush. I couldn't escape him, but I didn't want to either. My mind kept going back to what he'd said about us being joined by fate, and I bit my lip as I thought about what might have happened earlier if the other prytheen hadn't interrupted us.

What would those blue lips have felt like on mine?

"Lisa? Hello?" Maria waved her hand in front of my face, dragging me back from that flight of imagination, and my cheeks burned.

"Sorry," I said again. "Lack of sleep, I'm not focusing well."

A bright grin spread across Maria's pale face and she shook her head. "It looked like you were focusing well enough, just not on me," she said and chuckled. "I have drifted off like that daydreaming about my Alex often enough to recognize the look on someone else. But who is it that has you so distracted?"

"No one!" I blinked, swallowing and trying to get my emotions under control. The rush of embarrassment made it hard to think. "I mean, um…"

She laughed, raising an eyebrow and tilting her head to the side. "Come now, Lisa, there aren't *that* many options here. Aside from you and your brother there are only seven humans to pick from. It's not me or Alex, obviously. Mr. Carrington is too old for you… so. David? He's near your age, and I suppose not bad looking."

She laughed again, not unkindly. I wanted to melt

into the floor as she interrogated me, but I forced myself to shake my head.

"It's not him, and I don't want to talk about it." I tried to be stern about it. "It doesn't matter, not right now. I came here to help you with the rover, not get the Spanish Inquisition."

Maria pulled a disappointed face but relented, waving me over to the workstation. "Fine, don't tell me. I need a hand with these links, this is really a two-person job.

"But we aren't done with this conversation. I will find out who your crush is."

Not if I can help it, I thought as I called up Henry to show me the rover's instruction manual. The little hologram hopped up onto a crate to supervise and I glared at the amused expression on his fluffy virtual face.

"This isn't funny," I told him as the manual unfolded in the air above him. He cocked his translucent head to the side, mouth hanging open in silent laughter, and I glared at him. I couldn't keep that up for long — it's not easy to stay annoyed with a Pomeranian puppy. Henry was simply too cute.

The work was no easier than farming, but it was different enough to be something like a break. Between us, Maria and I got the frame assembled and the motor and batteries attached. In an emergency that would be enough to drive but given the hostile environment we wanted to have something more solid between us and the Crashland wildlife.

"Break time," Maria said, stepping back to look at what we'd achieved with some pride. "The rest will be quick and easy."

"Thank god," I said, grabbing a bottle of water and taking a long swig. "Not easy enough though."

The rover's modular design meant that the remaining sections should simply bolt together. The instructions Henry helpfully displayed showed me just how easy it would be to put on a passenger section, but that still meant the two of us moving a lot of weight. Not just the frame of the vehicle itself, but the three stasis tubes we still had to load.

Even with the ceiling-mounted hoist to help, thinking about the work we had ahead of us made my muscles ache and I groaned, rubbing my arms.

Maria's eyes twinkled as she took her own drink. "I know how to take your mind off the work," she said. "Just think about Stephen."

She'd timed her comment perfectly, nearly making me spit out the mouthful of water as I reacted. The middle Carrington brother? Ew. David was a creep, but his younger brothers were no better.

Maria's mirth faded as she watched my reaction, and she shook her head in disappointment. "Not Stephen, then? Louis?"

I shook my head quickly, finally managing to swallow. "No, damn it. None of the Carringtons."

Which... ruled out everyone. Every male human aside from her husband, anyway. Maria frowned at me disapprovingly and I realized I'd backed myself into a corner.

"Okay, okay, I'll talk," I said, screwing the cap back on my water bottle with unnecessary violence. "But if you laugh at me, I'll throw this at you."

Beside me Henry barked a warning at Maria and she nodded, face solemn but eyes twinkling. This was the gossip she'd wanted.

I sighed. "It's not one of us at all. It's Torran."

There. I'd said it out loud. I had a crush on an alien. I looked at the floor, unwilling to meet Maria's eyes.

To her credit, she didn't laugh. Didn't exclaim in horror either. Instead she let out a low whistle.

"The alien you shot?" The crate shook as she hauled herself up beside me, shooing Henry out of the way. Her own hologram monkey perched on top of the half-assembled rover, watching as Maria considered me carefully. "Is that wise, Lisa?"

"Probably not," I admitted. "But I can't keep my mind off him. And he's been nothing but good to me. If it wasn't for him I'd be dead — Arvid nearly killed me that first night."

Maria shook her head. "That does not mean much, you know. You were only in danger because they attacked us."

"Sure, but..." I trailed off, throwing up my hands in frustration. I hadn't taken the time to consider my feelings and trying to unpack them in front of someone else wasn't easy. "Look, he cares. I can feel it, I see it in his eyes. If he was a bad man, he's had enough chances taken his revenge, right? He wouldn't be helping me escape."

"And if he was a good man, perhaps you wouldn't *have to* escape," Maria said, squeezing my shoulders. "He could have come in peace and not helped conquer us."

I shrugged at her uncomfortably, wishing I had better answers to offer. She had a point. How much could I trust the alien man who'd led the attack that captured us?

How can I doubt him? He's killed one of his own to protect me. "I don't know what to think. But I know I can trust him, and if I'm wrong about that none of us are getting out of here."

Maria cocked her head to the side, considering. Then she sighed. "We are already trusting him with our lives, Lisa. Be careful if you trust him with your heart too. All of these aliens are a danger to us, please remember that. Once we're free… I do not want my Tania near any of them. Not even your Torran."

I couldn't argue, not with what the prytheen had put her family through. What would that mean for Torran, though? Would my fellow humans drive him off, or worse? I didn't want to think about it, but I couldn't put it off forever. Even if the others let Torran travel with us, what would happen once we were safely away from here? We'd be looking for a human settlement, and Torran might not be welcome there. Might, in fact, be shot on sight.

That's how I'd reacted to seeing him. It wouldn't be fair to blame someone else for doing the same.

All of that was a problem for tomorrow, though: if we didn't escape none of it would matter. I picked up a wrench and walked back to the half-assembled rover, looking at Henry for the instructions. He bounced closer, happy to help.

"What happens after he helps us escape can wait till we're safely away. Right now, we won't get far without him. And we're not going anywhere without the rover."

Maria hopped down behind me, put a comforting hand on my shoulder, and let out an unhappy breath. "A fair point. I just... I don't want you getting hurt, once this is over and we're at the valley. None of us know what will happen then, but it may not be good for you to get too attached to Torran."

I swallowed, images flashing through my mind. Torran, gunned down or driven off just as we reached our new home. What would I do then?

No. I just said I don't have to think about this yet, so I won't. Once we're safe from Gurral and his thugs, that's when I'll worry about this.

With the sinking feeling that I'd simply put off the heartbreak for later, I helped Maria bolt the side panels on the rover. At least we had a lot of work to distract me from my fears.

14

TORRAN

*W*alking around in the open air was a relief after the long days recovering in sickbay, and I reveled in it. The scents of Crashland were still strange to me, and the alien grasses underfoot made me feel alive.

Most of the Silver Band lived aboard their ships and didn't mind the confined spaces, but I was a scout. I lived to explore strange planets, to see new life. And for far too long I'd been cooped up in one small room. If I ever got the chance to tell my tale to the rest of the clan, they'd laugh at me.

Well, so be it. Locked in a small room with my khara tending to my wounds — it *was* an amusing mix of good luck and bad.

I roamed out, past the ultrasonic fence that kept the planet's wildlife at bay, trying to get used to this world again. Soon I'd have to lead Lisa and the other humans through this terrain, and at the moment, every other prytheen knew the area better than I did. One day wouldn't change that but I had to do what I could.

A game trail wound through the woods near the camp, possibly large enough for the humans' rover. That was both good and bad — it would be faster to travel this way, but easy to follow too. Still, speed would be more important, and any other route would mean pushing through the undergrowth blindly.

What kind of animal makes a trail this size? It had to be something big, and that worried me. Alone it would make for an interesting challenge, but I didn't look forward to running into whatever it was while I had humans to protect. Right now it was clear, with no signs of recent passage. Perhaps we'd be lucky and wouldn't have to face whatever it was.

I bit back a bitter laugh. My luck didn't seem that good these days.

Turning aside into the underbrush, I set myself the task of finding something to eat. I'd relied on others feeding me for too long and that wouldn't do for a scout.

The bright pale sun had passed its zenith by the time I returned to the little colony carrying my kill. A large herbivore, its hide covered in fine, razor-sharp spines, it had been an invigorating challenge to hunt with only my knives. Proof I'd recovered from my injuries.

I stepped out of the woods and saw the humans hard at work in the fields. Good, nothing to attract attention there. The cluster of prytheen guards paid them barely any attention, speaking amongst themselves in hushed tones.

Their body language told me there was a problem. Suspicious eyes looked my way the moment I emerged from the trees, and then they turned away again. Whatever the guards were talking about, they were anxious and agitated.

Had they discovered something about the escape? Arvid was with them, and I hoped I'd get some answers from him. I made my way over to them, dropping my prey's carcass with a thump that drew their attention.

"What's wrong?" I asked, looking from one to the next with my blankest expression. "You look like someone's stolen the keys to your ship."

The four of them snarled at me, anger and suspicion in their eyes. I didn't know the one who spoke up. "Have you seen Rarric?"

I hesitated only a moment, hiding a surge of relief. If they were looking for him, Lisa's nanites must have done their work and disposed of the body. "Not since last night. Why?"

"He's missing," Arvid said. "No one's seen him since yesterday, maybe not since you saw him."

I shrugged as casually as I could. "I took over his watch for him. He seemed keen to go, and he took a rifle. I think he went hunting? Is he not back yet?"

This was the first time I'd ever wished for talent at lying, but it had never been a skill the Silver Band excelled at. Layol's clan of manipulators were the exception, and they'd mostly used their abilities to keep the Band together and functioning. Not easy with a predator species like the prytheen, we needed someone to be the social glue if we were going to work in clans larger than a handful at a time.

Arvid frowned slightly, looking at me and the animal I'd brought back. "If he left last night, he's been out there a long time, and that's not like him."

The one who'd spoken first looked out at the trees, face darkening. His hands tensed, claws sliding from their sheathes. "I loved Rarric as a brother, but he is no hunter. That's why he took the dull watch duty; in all the cycles I've fought at his side, he's avoided wildlife. I can't imagine he'd choose to go hunting and if he did, he wouldn't go alone."

Sundered space. I tried to keep my dismay from showing. That shouldn't have been a surprise, but it had never occurred to me that Rarric might not like the outside. Most prytheen enjoyed hunting but some of us, used to our ships from living aboard them, disliked the open sky.

Rarric's friend watched me closely and I knew I'd have to say something, anything, to deflect suspicion. But if I called this man a liar, I'd provoke a fight I did not need. I shrugged again. "Rarric is a stranger to me, and I don't know why he wanted to swap shifts. Perhaps he wants to learn how to survive on a planet? It's not as though he has much choice about where to live now."

The warrior's eyes bored into me, searching. I met it evenly, not allowing myself to flinch. There was nothing to feel guilty about, I reminded myself. Yes, I'd killed a fellow warrior of the Silver Band, but he'd threatened my khara. He'd had to die.

"Come, Ervas," Arvid said, breaking the uncomfortable silence and placing a hand on the warrior's shoulder. "Whatever reason Rarric had for going out into the woods, he's been out there too long. We'd best search for him before it's too late."

Ervas scowled but broke eye contact with me. "Yes. *If* he's out there, we must find him. And if he's not—"

"Then we'll find out what happened to him," Arvid promised, leading him away and shooting a look at me. "Whatever it is, he cannot be far away. We'll solve this mystery."

I'd bought a little time, but not long. Before nightfall they'd be sure he hadn't left the colony, and at that point there'd be more questions for me. Nothing I could do about that now, though, so better not to dwell on it. I turned to the other warriors.

"Who here knows what I've caught and how to prepare it?" I asked, pointing to the animal I'd brought in. "I've never seen one of these before."

That turned the conversation back to more friendly territory, my fellow hunters congratulating me on my kill and telling me of their own. Tall tales and exaggeration followed, the old games of hunters talking about their greatest hunts, and I shared the companionship of my kind for what I feared might be the last time as we stripped the carcass and roasted it over an open fire.

It was delicious in the way only game I'd stalked

myself could be, and I told my own stories. Not of this hunt but of those on a dozen other planets, stories that none of these warriors could match. They tried, with good-natured lies about hunting animals twice their size 'armed only with a spear I crafted myself,' but we all knew it was nonsense.

By the time the sun dipped towards the horizon, other hunters returned to add to the haul. I looked carefully at the food they brought in, asking about their prey and making mental notes. Soon I might be reliant on hunting to feed not just myself but my khara too, and I wanted to learn everything Gurral's men had discovered about hunting the forests of Crashland. One thing they all agreed on was that the wildlife here was dangerous, and most of them would only hunt in pairs. I hid my frustration at that — it made my lies about Rarric that much less believable, but there was nothing I could do about that now.

Arvid and Ervas were the last to return, empty-handed and scowling. "No sign of Rarric anywhere," Arvid said. "No tracks, no blood, no corpse. Are you *sure* he went hunting, Torran?"

"I am not," I said, offering him a plate laden with roast meat. "He spoke of going hunting, but I didn't see him leave."

The smell of cooking meat brought the other prytheen out to join us, and I found myself in the middle of Gurral's warriors. News of Rarric's disappearance spread around the circle and I saw suspicious eyes turn towards me. Not good, not good at all. In an even, honest fight I'd take on any of these warriors, but I doubted that they would give me that chance if they thought I'd slain their companion.

These weren't honorable warriors, and I had to remind myself of that. They claimed the Code of the Silver Band guided them, but when it came time to test that, they'd discarded the inconvenient parts as fast as a hyper jump.

Am I any better? I frowned at the question, trying to push it aside for later. What would I have done if Lisa hadn't shot me? Would I have joined in the attack and enslavement of the humans, along with Arvid and the rest? Just thinking about it brought to mind Lisa's face, her brown eyes gazing up at me filled with fear.

Guilt stung my soul at the thought and I forced my attention back to the present. There was danger all around me and I had to be vigilant.

"What if the humans killed him?" I didn't see who asked the question and I kept quiet. If I spoke, it would be impossible to hide my anger — his accusation threatened Lisa's life, even if he didn't realize it.

"Impossible," Tarva answered. "They're no threat to us, just look at them. Small and weak creatures, without guns they can't harm a prytheen."

Glad someone else had taken up that gauntlet, I bit down on an urge to defend the honor of my khara's species. Better that they thought her and her kind harmless, even if that was an insult to the strength Lisa had shown.

Hopefully anyone who saw my expression would

read it as embarrassment over being shot by a human. That was at least partially true.

"Anyone is a threat if you don't keep your guard up." Gurral's voice broke through the discussion, silencing everyone. All eyes turned to him as he strode out of the shadow of the colony pod. He'd been watching, listening, waiting for a moment to make his appearance.

"Whatever happened to Rarric, we *will* find him," the leader continued. "If a human killed him, well, we won't need these humans for long. Some we can trust, but the rest... we'll have plenty of new humans to replace them soon. Won't we, Torran?"

Eyes turned towards me and I nodded, trying to look enthusiastic. "I'll find us a path into the human settlement, Gurral. Don't worry."

"I'm not worried," he said easily, his body language casual and relaxed. Only his eyes gave away his suspicions, boring into my soul. "I know that you'll get us in, and then we'll be safe and secure."

"Unless we bring a killer with us," someone else said. "No human can kill one of us in a fair fight but working together... we should kill these ones to be safe."

The murmur of agreement that followed made my blood freeze, but Gurral raised a hand and silence fell instantly. At least he had authority over his followers — that was something.

"If some of them slew Rarric, we'll figure it out," he assured them. "Don't worry, my friends, I will not take any chances. Humans are tricky beasts, not warriors like us. We'll only bring those we are certain we can trust with us. Beginning tomorrow, I shall question all the humans I have any doubts about. If they had anything to do with Rarric's disappearance, I'll find out."

A threat and a promise in one. To reassure his followers, Gurral would kill the other humans, but he couldn't touch my khara or suggest that she was to blame. I'd have laughed if it wasn't so horrible: my beloved was safe, but her fellows weren't — even though she was the one who'd attacked Rarric.

And the other humans would give up Lisa. I had no doubt of that: Gurral's questioning would be brutal but effective, and he'd break even the bravest of humans. If he interrogated them before we left, he'd discover the escape plan.

That settles it, I told myself. *We have to get out of here tonight.*

15

LISA

The prytheen talked loudly outside the pod as the rest of the humans filed in, weary from a day's work. Every one of my muscles ached and I longed for a solid night's rest, but with my nerves jangling like this I knew I couldn't expect one. I felt as though I'd had a dozen cups of coffee and despite my exhaustion, sleep was a thousand miles away.

But the rover was complete. Hopefully, anyway. Maria and I had checked and double-checked it. Henry had bounced around it, comparing the finished device to the blueprints. He was satisfied we'd done everything right, and it was his job to keep me safe. I tried to trust his programming.

All the diagnostics Maria ran told us the rover was good to go. Logging in through my wristband, I double checked. The remote diagnostics said everything was in working order and ready to go. Even the navigation system worked, though without a map of Crashland all it would be able to do was map where we'd been. We'd have to find our own path, or rather Torran would.

I wished we could turn the engine on and test the damned thing. That was out of the question, though: the battery took forever to charge and while it was plugged into the pod's power supply the hover engine wouldn't start. As a safety feature that made sense, but I didn't like it.

It'll work, I told myself. *It has to work.*

Testing was irrelevant anyway. If our heavy landing had broken part of the rover, we were trapped: there was no time to do any actual repair work. That didn't make the suspense any easier to bear though, and I longed to get under way.

Maria looked at our handiwork dubiously, her hologram monkey perched on her shoulder after making his own inspection. "When do you think we'll leave?"

"I don't know," I admitted. "Sooner rather than later, I expect. We should get something to eat."

As soon as I said it, I realized I hadn't eaten all day. Nutrient paste made from trees had never sounded as good. The matter processor doled out our scant rations into small bowls and we ate as we walked back to our quarters.

The other humans had already gathered there, looking frightened and unhappy enough that I was glad the prytheen didn't know how to read human body language. Someone who knew how to read our mood would have known we were up to something immediately.

Maria embraced her husband and daughter, whispering in German to them, leaving me to face the Carringtons.

David Carrington was the first to speak, holding up a bowl of unappetizing goop. "We, uh, we saved as much food as we can spare."

I smiled, surprised and touched. He wasn't coming along on our escape but he'd still done what he could to help the rest of us. Not like his father, who just glared at me.

"Thank you, David," I said, taking his offering. "That will be a big help."

He grinned and nodded, but before he had the chance to say anything more, the door slid open behind me. Everyone froze, and we couldn't have looked more guilty if we'd tried.

A large blue hand landed on my shoulder and squeezed. I relaxed instantly, recognizing Torran's gentle touch, and Maria stifled a giggle that made me want to glare at her. But at least it broke the tension of the moment and the other humans turned away, pretending to be very interested in something other than the alien warrior in our midst.

I turned and looked up at Torran. Even given the circumstances he didn't look happy. "What is it? Is something wrong?"

His gaze flickered across the room quickly before settling on me again. "We have to leave tonight. Tomorrow will be too late."

I didn't know whether to feel scared or relieved. At least it meant an end to the tension of waiting, but the reality of plunging into the darkness was terrifying. Even with a warrior like him to look after me.

"Now?" I asked, but he shook his head.

"Once the other prytheen are asleep," he said. "The slower they react the more likely we are to get away."

A shiver ran through me. I'd thought a lot about the dangers of traveling across this damned planet but the actual escape? I'd glossed over that in my mind.

Fortunately Torran hadn't. My alien warrior took everything into account, which meant we had a chance. But the idea of a running fight to get away still terrified me, and I put a hand on his broad chest to draw strength from him.

Maybe Carrington has a point, I thought, shooting the man a glance. *Staying's deadly for Malcolm, but for him? It might be safer to stay and trust Gurral's mercy.*

That still meant accepting slavery, though, and I wouldn't do that. Not even if my brother was safe here, and he wasn't. Alex and Maria weren't about to accept slavery for themselves or their daughter, either. My resolve firmed up as I looked at the three of them. *It's not just me and Malcolm, it's the Dietrichs too. We've got to get out of here.*

"Okay," I said to Torran, setting an alarm on my

wristband. If I somehow managed to drift off, I didn't want to risk sleeping through to dawn and missing our chance. "Later tonight, then. We've gathered all the supplies we can."

Not much, but it would have to do. Torran nodded, placing his hand on mine and squeezing gently. I felt better immediately. "You will be safe, my khara. Do not worry. If you need more food on the journey, I will hunt for you."

"Is there anything else we can do to prepare?" I asked him. He nodded again.

"I must see your vehicle, now that it is built," Torran said. "The better I know what I'm working with, the better a chance we have."

Hearing that, Maria jumped to her feet. I waved her back down. "At least one of us ought to get some rest, and you should spend time with Tania before we leave."

She raised an eyebrow and grinned, and a flush spread across my cheeks. "If you want to show him the rover alone, I won't stop you," she said. "I do need my sleep. But take care and remember what we talked about."

I nodded wordlessly, not trusting what I might say if I spoke. *She's worried about me,* I reminded myself. *That's a good thing, right?*

∿

TORRAN and I made our way down to the engineering

bay quickly and quietly, staying out of sight. Once we were inside, he shut the door and turned to me.

"What did the other human say?" he asked. "It made you uncomfortable."

"Nothing," I said, too fast. My blush deepened as I realized just how alone we were. This wasn't like the time in sickbay where he'd been my patient. Here he towered over me, strong and powerful, and my pulse raced as I bit my lip.

The room was soundproofed so that work here wouldn't disturb people living in the pod. No one would hear anything that happened in here. That thought made my breath catch as I looked up at the blue-skinned alien standing so tantalizingly close.

A second later he stepped back, a sharp, sudden movement. He'd felt the same pull I did, I knew it, but he wasn't giving in to his desire. And neither would I, I told myself.

"Here. The rover. It's ready to go." I pointed at the vehicle, feeling a little foolish. It wasn't as though he could miss it. But Torran seemed grateful for the excuse to look at something else, examining the white body of the rover with a careful, cautious gaze.

"Not well camouflaged," he said at last. "And it's large, too large for comfort. It will not be easy to hide its trail."

I tried to keep my temper under control. "It's not meant to be a military vehicle, you know. Being spotted easily was a feature for the Arcadia Colony."

"Here it might be a death sentence," Torran said distantly, turning his attention to the door seals. The rover didn't have its own air supply, but it did have filters and he nodded approvingly at the door's tight fit. I watched, feeling foolish. It wasn't like I needed his approval.

He examined the rover with a thoroughness that took time, looking everywhere, hands running over the curves of its hull. I felt a pang of something as I watched. Jealousy? That was ridiculous. How could I be jealous of a vehicle?

But it was hard not to wish he was giving *me* that thorough inspection instead.

"It will serve," he said at last, and I put my hands on my hips, glaring at him.

"Oh, I suppose you'd do better?"

A grin flashed across his face, gone as fast as it appeared. "If my technology worked, Lisa, I would whisk you away on wings of fire and show you the galaxy."

"But since it doesn't, you should be a little nicer about mine, which does." I frowned, trying not to show the way my heart skipped a beat at his words. Torran dropped down from the rover, stalking closer, and I stood my ground as my heart raced.

A sparkle in his eyes, Torran stood just too close for comfort. I repressed an urge to lick my lips nervously, keeping up my glare.

"You are right," he purred. That was the only word

for it, a sound no human voice could make. It sent a delightful shiver across my skin. "This is what we have, and I am grateful for it."

I swallowed. Took a deep breath and a step forward. Closer to him. "We have to go soon."

He nodded, golden eyes gleaming in the dim light. The intensity of his gaze burned into me, setting something in my soul on fire, and I froze. Torn between the impulse to move closer and the knowledge that I shouldn't.

I should keep my distance. Keep myself safe. Stay away from the dangerous alien predator.

The trouble was, I didn't want to.

I might have stood there forever, torn between two impulses, but Torran was more decisive. He moved so fast I hardly saw him, stepping close and sweeping me up in his arms. The air left my lungs in a loud gasp, a shiver ran through my body, and my back hit the wall with a thump as Torran pressed himself against me.

His arms felt strong, comforting, powerful. His heartbeat, strong and steady, echoed through me where our chests pressed together. His strange alien skin felt so different to a human's.

I tried to say something, but nothing more than a whimper came out. Torran looked into my eyes, his face inches from mine, and growled softly.

It wasn't a threat, or if it was, I wanted him to deliver on it. My heart raced and my teeth dug into my lip as I struggled for some kind of self-control.

"This may be our last night alive," he said, voice low

and strong and deep. "And I will not waste it on hesitation."

His mouth lowered to mine, a powerful kiss sending tremors through me. My lips parted in an eager moan as he took what we both wanted, his tongue pressing against mine, probing, exploring. Almost without me thinking about it, my arms wrapped around him and pulled him close.

Torran didn't need any more encouragement, lifting me and kissing with a fierce passion that drove all thought from me. My body ached for him, needed him, with a desperate fire I'd kept hidden from myself. Now that we touched, I couldn't deny it any longer.

When at last he broke our kiss, I gasped for air. But I wanted his touch more than I wanted to breathe, more than anything, and I struggled for some semblance of control as I looked up at him.

His grin revealed sharp teeth, predator's teeth, and his eyes burned with a need that frightened and excited me. The idea of being hunted by a man like this... I moaned again, leaning in to kiss his neck, biting gently.

That made him shudder, arch his back, tense against me. Strong hands squeezed me, and his claws slid out, sharp even through my clothes.

"If this is our last night, let's make it something to remember," I whispered, not sure if he'd hear, if he'd understand. Then I bit his neck, my teeth digging into tough prytheen skin, and he gasped and pulled me back.

The wild look in his eyes, the easy strength with

which he held me, the powerful hunger that burned in him — all of it sent shivers of need and lust through me as he turned and pinned me to the side of the rover, clawed hands pulling at my top. The fabric parted easily, his claws tearing fastenings he didn't understand, and in moments he pulled it from me.

I panted breathlessly as Torran stepped back to admire me, a blush spreading across my face, down to my now-bare breasts. The urge to cover up was strong, almost overwhelming.

But when I moved to raise my arms, Torran growled a warning and I stopped. Froze. His eyes devoured me, a careful examination that left no doubt how much he wanted me, how much he enjoyed the sight of me. If I'd needed any confirmation, the bulge in his pants made it perfectly clear.

He whispered a word I didn't know, voice deep and almost worshipful. Reached out for me again. I stepped aside, moved out of his reach while smiling and blushing brighter, shaking my head and pointing at him.

Turnabout was fair play. If he got to look at me...

It only took Torran a moment to understand, and then he laughed happily, pulling off his tunic and casting it aside. His bare chest rippled with muscles, the faint dark pattern on his blue skin almost hypnotic as he breathed. And his abs — my gaze drifted down and I licked my lips as saw his perfectly defined muscles, the vee that led down further.

His scars only made him sexier. Whatever threats had marked his body had done nothing to hurt his sex appeal. He'd overcome them, ending up stronger and smarter and oh so much hotter in the process. I reached out for the fastenings of his pants, wanting to see more of him, but this time he shook his head, grabbing my wrist and stopping me.

The touch of his hand held me still, frozen, a cascade of sensation rushing through me as he stepped closer. I tried to pull back, to get free — not that I wanted to succeed. He kept his grip easily, grinning as he pulled my arm over my head, pinned me to the rover, held me in place.

I grinned back, my chest heaving as my breath sped up. With my free hand I grabbed for him, but his reflexes were too quick, his grip too sure. Catching my wrist he dragged it up, pinning both my arms with one hand. Leaving me helpless. Trapped.

His.

I shivered at the touch of his free hand, feeling the brush of his claws as he trailed them down my arm, over my shoulder, across my chest. Pressing with just enough pressure that the sharp points dug in, but not enough to hurt or scratch. My breath caught, my eyes widened, and I bit back a cry as his fingers teased my breasts, circling, brushing my nipples.

Arching against him, I urged him on, but he was in no rush. Torran had me at his mercy and he intended to make the most of it. Lowering his mouth for another kiss, he swallowed my cries and drew his hand down, claws scratching deliciously, on the edge between pleasure and pain, until he reached the waistband of my pants.

"Oh god," I whimpered as he broke the kiss again, a smug, catlike smile on his lips as his fingers tugged the pants lower. My mind melted under waves of lust and I struggled against him, but his grip was too strong, too powerful. Inescapable.

A tug, and the fastenings of my pants parted, Torran's claws tearing them open as though they weren't there. I kicked off my boots, squirmed out of my pants as he tore them from me, and then I was naked.

Pinned to the side of the rover, bare before an alien predator, and loving it. My cheeks heated at the thought, but there was no guilt. This felt *right* in a way I wouldn't have been able to imagine before meeting Torran. I needed him, needed his touch.

Desperate, I pushed forward, arching to press myself to him. He chuckled, kissing my lips, my neck, my breasts, sharp teeth scraping my skin to make me cry out.

No. Not going to let you have all the fun. As much as I loved being helpless in his hands, I needed more. I ducked my head, kissing his neck, then bit down hard. Torran gasped, his hold loosening for a second, and that let me pull away, twisting out of his grip.

Laughing breathlessly, I ran. And made it all of two

steps before he was on me, pouncing and scooping me up. His arms wrapped around me from behind, pulling my naked body back against him, and his hardness pressed against me.

"You don't get away," he growled, that sexy voice making me shiver as he lifted me. But I wasn't struggling. My hands reached back, pulling at the unfamiliar fastenings of his pants until they fell open.

"Who says I want to go anywhere?" I asked, wriggling back against him and feeling him swell. He growled, hands squeezing and exploring, and I shuddered as my hand closed on his cock.

It swelled in my grip, alien texture strange and enticing under my fingers. And then it *buzzed*, vibrating powerfully enough to make me gasp in shocked surprise.

Torran chuckled, pushed me face down against the rover, growled into my ear. One hand slid down between my legs, parting them, fingers brushing across my pussy oh-so-delicately. My body responded instantly, a wave of pleasure and need washing away every conscious thought as his teasing touch drove me wild.

A finger parted my folds, rubbing firmly but gently, making me whimper and moan. I matched his speed, stroking the massive shaft of his cock as he pushed me to the rover and drove me closer, ever closer, to an orgasm.

"Mine," he growled into my ear, and bit down on

my shoulder. Sharp teeth dug in, my body arched as his fingers rubbed faster and faster, and I screamed as my orgasm ripped through me. Everything melted away in wave after wave of white light, and I would have collapsed if Torran hadn't held me up.

"Oh god," I whimpered as I managed to recover, twisting around to look into his golden eyes. "That was amazing."

His smile lit up his stern face, and he kissed me firmly on the lips. A tingle ran through my body again and I realized he wasn't done with me yet. Could my body take any more?

I fumbled at the rover's side door, sliding it open to reveal the spacious interior, padded for comfort during a rough ride. Which was exactly what I hoped Torran would give me.

He lifted me again, firmly but gently lifting me into the vehicle and parting my legs. Bracing myself, I moaned as I saw his hard cock. So big, bigger than I'd imagined even when I held it. And those ridges! I shivered at the delicious thought of them inside me and knew that I needed it more than I could say.

Torran didn't keep me waiting this time, climbing on top of me while covering me in kisses and little bites. I reached up to pull him to me, fingers digging into the muscles of his back and urging him on as his cock pressed against my opening.

"Please," I moaned, flushing again as I heard the pleading tone in my voice. His smile appeared again, a delighted grin as he gazed down at me.

And thrust.

The sensation was incredible, unbelievable. Torran slid into me with a single smooth motion, his powerful body slamming me into the padding of the rover. I'd never felt anything so perfect — he fit me like a key to a lock, a perfect union that sent me into writhing, gasping ecstasy.

A growl, and he drew back, leaving me empty and aching for a moment before he slammed home again. And again. And *again*, each time faster, harder, more powerful. Each time making me cry out, until my throat was hoarse and my body shook. My fingers clutched at him, pulling him closer, urging him on as he pounded into me.

My body shook with pleasure, my nerves alight with it as Torran drove me on and on. His cock, his wonderful alien cock, filled me more perfectly than anything I'd ever imagined — and then it started to vibrate inside me.

That was too much. I arched under him, screaming as I came in an endless wave of ecstasy that melted the whole world around me. I couldn't breathe, couldn't think, couldn't do anything aside from feel him inside me. My body convulsed around him, and I pulled him over the edge too. With a roar that drowned out my cries, Torran came inside me, filling me, completing me.

Spent, panting, we collapsed together, my arms wrapped around my alien lover. There was no space for deception now, no distance between us, and I couldn't deny it to myself.

I was his, he was mine. We belonged together.

Snuggling into his arms, I rested my head on his chest.

You'd better not die tomorrow, I thought as the darkness claimed me.

16

TORRAN

Resting in my khara's arms was the best feeling in this or any other world. As far as I'd traveled, as much as I'd seen of the universe, I'd experienced nothing like the wonder of Lisa's body pressed against me. She rested, breathing slow and even, one arm flung across me and her head resting on my chest.

I should sleep too, I thought. *Gather strength for the coming fight.* But the idea of wasting these moments when they might be the only ones I'd ever share with my khara was ridiculous. I had one chance to savor her presence, one night to remember her by.

If I died protecting her, I wanted the memory of tonight burned into my soul. Something to keep me warm in the cold dark of death.

Lisa muttered something, shifting her weight restlessly, and I stroked her hair. Soft, smooth, a delight to the touch.

She murmured happily and stilled, relaxing again. Perfect.

I don't know how long we lay there, intertwined. It wasn't long enough. All too soon, the hologram puppy appeared beside her, barking and nuzzling at her.

It took an effort to resist the urge to smash the emitter. It was right — we had to go now if we wanted a hope of escaping.

"What is it?" Lisa asked sleepily, blinking awake. The play of emotions across her face was a delight to watch, starting with sleepy confusion, moving through embarrassment and then delight as she remembered the night. Only then did reality hit, and she sat up abruptly, looking at her hologram.

"You shouldn't have let me sleep," she said accusingly. I chuckled.

"You set an alarm. I'd rather have gnawed off my arm than wake you before it did," I told her. "And you needed the rest. This will be a long day."

The hologram whined and Lisa reached out for it, scratching behind its virtual ears. Something about the tiny mammal made me relax. An ultrasonic effect, or simply cuteness? Did it even matter?

My khara muttered words in her own language to the hologram, and glyphs appeared between its ears. She glowered at them and then sighed.

"I wish we had more time," she said, the comfort of our time together fading as quickly as morning mist. I sighed, rolling up and grabbing my clothes.

Hers were ruined, torn to shreds and scattered

around the room. My impatience with their fastenings hadn't left much to salvage, and Lisa didn't waste time trying. She grabbed a spare outfit from a box in the corner, pulling them on quickly while I watched transfixed by her beauty.

Noticing me, she tried to glare. Her blush and little smile spoiled the effect and were nearly enough to tempt me into tearing the fresh clothes off her. *Patience, Torran,* I counseled myself. *We'll have plenty of time together, no need to rush things now.*

That assumed we both survived the day but delaying our escape wouldn't make that more likely.

Once Lisa had stamped her feet into her boots, she made her way to the door and opened it, peeking cautiously into the dim corridors of the colony pod. I tensed, wondering what waited for us out there. The other prytheen had been suspicious enough that Gurral might have set extra sentries. Was she sticking her head into a trap?

I wouldn't let Lisa take that chance. Holding her back, I stalked out into the corridor, listening for any sign of movement. Nothing. It was as quiet as a tomb. So far, so good.

"Stay with the rover," I said, holding up a hand as Lisa tried to follow me out. "Get it ready to go while I fetch the other humans. If any other prytheen comes, don't wait for us. Just get out of here and get to safety."

She didn't look happy at the suggestion, and I didn't blame her. I didn't want to separate us either — but if something went wrong with the plan, at least with the rover she had some small chance of escape. Not a *good* chance, but far better than the rest of us would have.

"You stay, I'll go," she countered, crossing her arms and glaring at me defiantly. "The others won't listen to an alien."

"They had better, because I'm going," I replied. Her defiance might have been amusing under other circumstances, but we had no time for it now. "I cannot get the rover ready to leave, and I do not know how to drive it. You will have to prepare it."

Her glower deepened, but she had no answer to that. Thank the ancestors, because I couldn't bear the thought of her walking deeper into the pod, perhaps into a trap. I turned away, but her hand caught my tunic and pulled me back.

"Wait," Lisa said, fumbling at her wrist and taking off the band with the hologram emitter. "Take Henry, that way they'll know I sent you. And don't you dare get yourself killed doing this. I don't want to lose you."

Before I could respond, she stepped close and kissed me. Her soft lips planted a promise on mine, and a shiver ran through me as we parted. I had no words, so I nodded and snatched the wristband, turning before my feelings for my khara overcame me.

Why couldn't we simply go, vanish into the night? We would be long gone by the time anyone followed, and I'd cover our trail too well for anyone to follow. Even bringing her brother, we'd move fast enough to vanish into the woods.

But I knew better than that. Lisa would no more

abandon her people than I would mine if the situation were reversed. As different as my khara was from me, in that we were alike.

~

THE POD ECHOED empty around me and I breathed a little easier as I found the door to the humans' barracks unguarded. After the suspicious way the others had spoken earlier, I'd worried that there might be more security to deal with. But no, Gurral wasn't willing to force more guard duty on his men.

He might regret that tomorrow.

I took a quick detour on the route to the humans' cell, stopping by sickbay and retrieving the rifle I'd hidden there. It was a risk, coming that close to the armory guard, but our need for a weapon outweighed the chance of getting caught.

No one saw me. Perhaps fate had decided to bless me. Or perhaps it was setting me up for a bigger fall later. I didn't trust luck.

The way to cell was clear and the door slid open silently. Inside, the humans looked up at me with a start. All of them were awake, even those that weren't going, and I wondered if any of them regretted that decision. If so, this was their last chance to change their minds.

Even if Gurral spared their lives, anyone who stayed wouldn't get another chance.

"It is time," I said. "Come with me as quietly as you can."

"Now hold on everyone," the red-faced oldest male human said, holding back the others. "How do we know this isn't a trap? For all we know you've already killed Lisa and you're testing our loyalty."

I growled, frustrated and annoyed. Resisting the urge to grab his outstretched finger, I narrowed my eyes and replied. "If I wanted to kill you, I wouldn't need an excuse. Gurral wouldn't blink an eye. I am only here because Lisa wants to save as many of you as possible. And she gave me this to show I come from her."

The wristband buzzed as I held it up and Henry appeared in my arms. I glared over the holographic bundle of fluff, looking at the humans and daring them to doubt my word. The virtual animal barked twice, then turned and *licked* my face. Caught by surprise, I tried not to laugh at the sensation as the hologram's forcefield brushed across my skin. A weird, somehow-delightful sensation.

As undignified as it was, the display seemed to calm the humans. Malcolm held a hand over his mouth, muffling a laugh as I struggled to keep a straight face. The others all relaxed. The older man scowled, but that had settled the question of whether I was on Lisa's side.

"She will get you all killed," he grumbled, shaking his head. Switching to the human's language, he spoke sharply to those who gathered their supplies to follow me.

They didn't stop to argue, and soon four humans stood ready to leave. Another four stood back, the red-faced man and his sons. The Carringtons, I remembered the strange human name now.

The younger ones looked less certain than their father but the four of them stuck together. I had to respect that loyalty, even if I thought it misplaced and dangerous.

"This is your last chance," I said, addressing the human leader. "Once we leave, you will be stuck here at Gurral's mercy."

"Better that than dying in the forest," he snapped back. "We will be perfectly fine here."

I didn't argue further, shouldering the remaining pack — that had to be Lisa's. One last check that no one was watching the corridor, and then I led the other humans out into the pod.

The lighting was dim by my standards, and the humans seemed almost blind as they stumbled along behind me. I cursed under my breath, slowing to let them keep up and wincing at every sound. The guard at the armory could hear us at any moment, even if no other prytheen came inside.

Sundered Space, if we make it out of this, I'll be amazed. But luck or fate sided with us and somehow we reached the engineering bay and the waiting rover undetected. Malcolm leaped forward, throwing his arms around his sister in a quick embrace while the others loaded their supplies aboard.

The five humans packed the rover fast and got it

ready to move. One of them disconnected the power cable from the vehicle and, with an almost inaudible whine, the anti-grav field kicked in.

Primitive, like all human technology. It barely lifted the vehicle. But the important thing was that it worked. We had a chance.

"Which of you are going in the stasis tubes?" I asked. The five of them looked at each other, uncertain, and I grumbled. Had they not discussed that?

No time for any long debate. "Very well. Who here is the best driver?"

Malcolm's hand shot up and Lisa glared at her brother. No one argued, though. I gave them a second, then nodded.

"You and Lisa will remain awake," I told him, turning to the remaining humans. "You three, into stasis. We'll wake you when we've arrived."

They shared a look, the male going pale. Before I expressed my impatience, though, the older female grabbed his hand and practically dragged him to the back of the rover. She said something to him in a human language, not the English I'd learned a few words of but something harsher on the ears. After a moment he nodded.

"I have told him it is safe," she told him, switching to Galtrade. "We crossed the stars in stasis, a few more days won't hurt us. We are trusting you to get us all to safety. Don't fuck it up."

I felt the ghost of a smile on my face as I nodded. "I will do everything in my power to protect your family."

With the odds against us, it would be dishonest to promise more than that. I refused to lie to them, and I doubted that Maria would appreciate a comforting untruth anyway.

She hugged her daughter, lifted her into one of the stasis tubes and closed the lid. A green light came on and she sighed.

"I wish they didn't look so much like coffins," she said, running a hand over the sealed box. "Sleep well, Tania."

Lisa's arms enfolded me and we gave the two parents their privacy as they sealed themselves in. Despite Maria's brave words, she had to be frightened. They would sleep in stasis until they were woken, but that might never happen if we failed.

Without the support units on a colony pod, the passengers couldn't be revived. I shivered at the thought of saying goodbye to Lisa like that and didn't know if I had the strength for it. That was one reason I hadn't let her be one of the frozen passengers on this journey.

"Time to go," I told my khara once the Dietrichs were safely in their tubes. I lifted her into the rover's cabin, shooing Malcolm out of the driver's seat. He might be a skilled driver, but I would trust this to Lisa first.

She looked like she might say something, but no words came. Instead she pulled me close for a kiss, and I ignored her brother's disgusted noise as we embraced passionately for what might be the last time.

Parting from her, I went to the loading ramp controls. They were simple enough — press this button and the ramp would drop. Once I did that, we'd be in the hands of fate. Would any of Gurral's men see the ramp lower? How quickly would they respond? There was no way to tell. I didn't think much of their discipline, but they wouldn't have to be very alert to notice the vehicle leave.

I looked back at the rover, meeting Lisa's eyes through the windshield and seeing her fear and determination. For a moment we drew strength from each other, and then I hit the switch.

The ramp dropped fast, hitting the ground with a rattling thump loud enough to wake anyone nearby. I leaped out, ready to attack any prytheen unlucky enough to be immediately outside, but there was no one there.

Behind me, the rover leaped forward, engine roaring as it powered up. I jumped up to the hang onto its side as it rumbled past, the antigravity engine as loud as I'd expected. Even if they'd missed the thud of the ramp, there was no way the prytheen would miss this.

Before we could orient the vehicle, Myrok appeared around the colony pod, looking for the source of the sudden, unfamiliar noise. We saw each other at the same moment, and I threw a knife as he dove back into cover. The blade hit his shoulder rather than his throat, and his roar of pain filled the night.

Any attempt at stealth was futile now. I banged on

the windshield to get Lisa's attention and pointed in the direction of the game trail I'd seen. The rover bounced on the uneven terrain, Lisa stamping on the accelerator, and I clung on with one hand, unslinging the laser rifle with the other as we hurtled towards the trees. Behind us the howls of pursuit started, Gurral's followers waking in confusion and setting out after us.

In the farmland we were far too fast for a prytheen to run down, though the bumps threatened to tear my arm off. A knife clattered from the back of the rover, a spear whizzed past me, and I glanced back to see Myrok at the head of a band of warriors chasing us.

A feral grin pulled at my lips. If he caught up with us I'd enjoy tearing his heart out — he'd threatened my khara, would have killed her if I hadn't intervened. I owed him for that.

Getting away is more important than getting revenge, I reminded myself. If I could save Lisa but her tormentor survived, I'd take that bargain. But if someone was going to catch up to us, then let it be someone I already had reason to kill.

With a crack of ionized air, a laser bolt snapped past. Then another, closer, as the shooter adjusted his aim. Lisa hauled at the wheel, pulling the rover into a sharp turn that nearly threw me clear, and laser fire burned into the vehicle's hull.

I snarled back at our pursuers, raising my own rifle one-handed. Only two of them had lasers, but if they hit the engine, our escape attempt would end before it had properly begun. The trees were close, tantalizingly close, but the shots were landing too close for comfort.

Shooting from the back of the rover was a fool's game. Bouncing unsteadily, needing one hand to hang on, I'd never hit anything. I tried anyway, snapping shots in the vague direction of our pursuers and hoping to slow them down. It worked, a little — some of the hunters dropped to the ground to avoid my shots.

That wasn't enough. The shooters ducked but kept firing, and I knew with a gut-deep certainty that one of them would find their mark before we reached the safety of the tree line. I had to do something to stop them and shooting back wouldn't work.

Only one idea occurred to me, a desperate plan that might work. I looked at the human weapon in my hand. Flimsy construction, primitive power supply, and no targeting to speak of. It was the only ranged weapon we had, but what I needed was something else. Flipping it in my hand, I caught it by the battery and *squeezed*, feeling the plastic crack. Sudden heat burned my palm.

It had enough power for a hundred or more shots. Hoping that would be enough for what I had in mind, I threw it at the prytheen gunners with all my strength and closed my eyes.

The rifle spun through the air and I heard a sharp crack. Even through closed eyelids the flash of the battery exploding was blinding, and the howls of our pursuers turned into cries of pain. A final aimed shot snapped past me, close enough to feel the laser-light's heat on my skin. Then the shooters were reduced to firing blindly after us, their wild shots nowhere near the rover. I'd bought us precious seconds at the cost of our only firearm.

Moments later the rover lurched, slowing as Lisa brought it into the forest and amongst the undergrowth. Out of sight, safe for now, we raced away from the colony as fast as she dared drive. The rover burst through the ultrasonic fence and we were away.

Branches lashed my back as I clung to the side of the rover, but I didn't mind the sting. We'd survived, we'd escaped, and while Gurral would no doubt chase us, we could put distance between us and the enemy before they recovered enough to pursue.

For the first time, I let myself believe that this crazy plan might actually work.

17

LISA

The rover bucked under me as I steered it into the woods, Henry whining and covering his face with his paws. I clutched the steering wheel, my knuckles white, every muscle in my body taught. Somehow, I managed to pull the vehicle through the narrow gaps between trees and leave the colony behind.

The hover vehicle skimmed along faster than I was comfortable with, but I didn't dare slow down. We needed as much space between us and those angry prytheen as we could get.

My driving skills came back as I went, jinking around trees and bouncing over the rough terrain. I started to relax, loosening my death-grip on the wheel as I got my breathing under control.

This is easier than I thought it would be, I thought a little smugly. As though the universe wanted to punish me for that, a branch clipped the right-hand mirror off the side of the rover, and I squeaked.

Thankfully Torran was on the *left* side, or I might have scraped him off instead. Taking the hint, I slowed down to a more manageable pace, hoping that our pursuers wouldn't be able to catch up. With the trees between us, I had no idea how close they were.

A small price to pay for them not being able to shoot at us.

In the seat next to me, Malcolm uncurled from the tight, frightened ball he'd curled into, glancing at the trees flashing past us and whimpering. "Slow down, sis, you're going to get us killed."

"If I slow down any more, they'll catch up," I said, my voice tight. "Then we'll definitely get killed."

Maybe not the most reassuring line I could have gone with, but it had the virtue of being true. Malcolm whimpered again but turned to look out of his window and warn me when we were getting too close to the trees. It didn't actually help much, but at least he was trying.

Torran knocked on the window and I barely controlled a flinch that would have put us in a ditch. His quick gestures probably meant more to someone who'd learned the Silver Band's combat sign language, but one thing was clear. He was pointing out a direction.

Fine. It's not like I know where I'm going. And I knew enough about my directional skills to worry I'd drive in circles if I didn't have someone to navigate for me.

Not long after I started to follow his pointing, we broke free of the undergrowth onto a broad trail. Broad by some standards, at least. Barely wide enough for the rover, it still gave me a path to follow through the forest and that let me catch my breath.

I wound the window down, letting in the scents of the alien forest. Daring a quick glance at Torran, I saw him grinning at me and some of his exhilaration rubbed off.

This is crazy, we nearly died five times back there. I shouldn't be enjoying myself.

But we'd survived which made it all worthwhile. I took a deep breath and choked back a laugh. If I started I didn't know if I'd be able to stop, and that wouldn't be great while I was at the wheel. A crash would be the end of us.

"We did it," I said once I had control of myself. "I can't believe we really did it."

"We're not safe yet," Torran cautioned, but I heard the fierce elation in his voice. Reaching in through the open window he squeezed my shoulder and I grinned. Trees zipped past on either side of us, the headlights catching alien plants for brief moments.

The trail wound this way and that, but it ate the distance and after a while I felt safe slowing down. The adrenaline rush of the escape was wearing off and my hands started to shake on the wheel. No point risking damaging our only vehicle.

"I need a break," I said, slowing to a crawl and

turning to my brother. "Can you take a turn at driving?"

"Sure!" Malcolm answered, his eagerness almost amusing. He practically bounced in his seat, and I shook my head but stopped the rover. As soon we were stationary, I felt the tension I'd been ignoring — every muscle ached and my head swam.

It was amazing what I'd been able to ignore in the middle of the escape but now it all hit at once and I winced. Shutting down the engine, I pushed the door open and dropped down beside Torran. The dark forest around us seemed to eat the light, but it felt good to be out of the driver's seat.

"Okay, give me five minutes to stretch," I said. "Then you can take over, Malcolm."

I needed to move, to walk, to do something. My legs ached and my head swam as I moved to a tree and leaned against it. The rough, strange bark felt like nothing on Earth but I clung to it anyway. Something solid, something new. Something different from the colony and the farm.

In the forest, a light moved and I tensed up for a moment before realizing that it couldn't be our pursuers. Wrong direction, wrong kind of movement. Wrong kind of light too, a fluttery blue-green glow. Some kind of wildlife. There were pretty things on Crashland as well as dangers.

Torran's shadow fell over me as he stepped between me and the rover. I looked back at him, silhouetted against the lights. He stood silently watching me and I felt the powerful presence of him. My heart beat a little faster as he stroked my cheek.

"We're doing the right thing, aren't we?" The question came out without a conscious choice from me. I looked away, out into the darkness, listening to the wildlife rustling in the bushes. This was further into the wilderness than I'd ever been.

Torran folded me into a powerful hug, as though he was trying to squeeze the doubts out of me. "It is the only thing, my khara. And I will keep you safe."

Now I'd started speaking, though, it was hard to stop. I clung to Torran, my words muffled as I continued. "I just keep thinking, what if Carrington's right and I'm making a mistake? What if we die out here and never get to safety?"

"Nothing is certain," he said, and I shivered in his arms. "But you would not have been safer with Gurral. No one is safe with him, my khara. His ambition will ruin those close to him, no matter what they do."

Way to cheer a girl up! I tried to relax and to appreciate his honesty. I'd rather have the truth than false hope, but that didn't make it easy to swallow. "Will they follow us? Hunt us down? The trail we're on is easy to follow, right?"

Torran's chuckle vibrated through me. "He may try, but this is a dangerous forest and he has no one to scout for him. Once we leave the trail he'll have to slow down to follow our tracks. And blundering around in this forest will get him and his men killed if they aren't careful. Don't worry, my love, we'll stay ahead of him until we reach the valley."

I sighed and snuggled into him, the night air chilly around me. His words, his presence, his warmth, all comforted me. It was a lot easier to feel confident in his arms.

The fluttering light appeared again, close enough to let me make out what it was. A strange creature, something like a moth with luminous edges to its wings. I almost reached out to touch it before remembering I had no idea whether it was safe. Beautiful but deadly was a possibility, and we didn't have an autodoc with us, only the small selection of medicine I'd managed to steal. Finding out that those things had a deadly sting would be a hell of a way to end our escape.

Better to watch from a safe distance, I thought as I saw another and then another flutter out of the undergrowth.

I slid an arm around Torran's waist and sighed, leaning my head on his chest and listening to his strong heartbeat. Together we watched the glowing moths flutter in the darkness.

"I'm sorry you had to abandon your friends," I said. "And that the others don't recognize what you've given up for them."

"Khara, it doesn't matter. I would give up far more for your safety, and those who threatened you aren't my friends. I should never have helped Arvid in the first place."

We stood in silence, watching the glowing insects

flutter from tree to tree. There didn't seem to be anything else to say, but we didn't need words. Not when we had each other.

"Come on, we'd better get back," I said reluctantly after a minute or two had passed. "I want to get as much distance between us and Gurral as we can."

Torran nodded. "But you aren't driving," he said firmly. "Let Malcolm do that, you need your rest."

"You're not the boss of me," I said, then yawned and stretched with a laugh. "Okay, fine, I already asked him to take over. But you're tired too, so you come rest with me."

"I don't need— *ouch.*" He rubbed his ribs where I'd elbowed him and chuckled. "Fine."

We smiled at each other happily.

That was when we heard the roar.

I spun towards the noise, staring up the trail at the animal that had appeared. It was huge, bigger than I could take in. It filled the trail, four huge eyes glaring at us in confused anger, shaggy pelt white in the rover's lights. The creature's mouth opened wide for another deep roar that shook the ground, and part of me wondered how something that big had gotten that close without us noticing.

The rest of me was screaming internally. *Oh my fucking god it's a monster, it's going to eat us.* That mouth was huge, full of jagged teeth, and weird tentacles snapped out as it screamed a challenge at the rover and pawed the ground. Massive horns atop its head gleamed in the light. What did a behemoth like this need them for? What the *fuck* did it usually fight?

I stood frozen to the ground, unable to move. It took a moment for me to realize that the terrified whimper I heard came from my own throat. But Torran hardly paused. Without hesitating, he pulled me behind him, putting himself between me and harm. Challenging that monster armed only with knives might be a futile gesture, but he made it instantly.

And as frightened as I was, I couldn't help wondering if his confidence was justified. Did he really believe he could win?

18

TORRAN

I didn't see any way to beat this monster. That didn't mean I would let myself give up. I'd promised to defend my beloved to my dying breath, and that was what I'd do.

I spun towards the sound, putting myself between Lisa and danger. Ahead of us, caught in the rover's headlight, the alien beast screamed a challenge that shook the ground under my feet. It was huge, bigger than anything I'd hunted. Bigger than the rover itself.

So that's what made this trail. A part of my mind filed away the answer to that question, though I wished it had stayed a mystery. The huge animal filled the gap between the trees, its heavy head swinging from side to side as it tried to decide how to respond to the rover blocking its path.

Heavy horns jutted from either side of its head, points gleaming as they caught the light. Beady eyes peered past folds of heavy hide, tough-looking scales covered its neck, and as it roared another challenge it showed off huge teeth.

Crushing teeth, I thought, not meant for tearing flesh. A small mercy — this looked like a herbivore not a predator. It wouldn't kill us for food, but that didn't mean it would take a challenge to its territory well.

"Move slowly. Keep quiet. Get into the rover." I hissed the words to Lisa, keeping my eyes on the animal as it stepped forward and roared again. She let out a quick hiss of breath and I heard her take a step back. The creature's head snapped around, eyes glaring at the sound, and my blood ran cold.

If that thing charged her there'd be no stopping it. It probably weighed as much as the rover and would crush anything that got in its way. If I still had the rifle, then *maybe* I'd have been able to get a killing shot — but even then, it looked like I'd have to hit an eye to do a creature this size any damage.

Without a weapon,, I saw only one way to protect my khara. Not a good plan or a smart one, but that didn't matter. Not when her safety hung in the balance.

I stepped away from Lisa, waving my hands. The animal's gaze followed me, lowering its massive head and snorting. *Yes, that's right, look at me. If you've got an enemy here, I'm it.*

"Calm, beast, calm," I said, voice as low and soothing as I could manage. Keeping its attention was the important thing, but I'd rather not have to fight it. "We're just passing through, that's all. No need to fight, we don't want your territory."

Behind it, something moved. I could barely make out smaller shapes hiding in the shadow of the big creature and I winced. A mother protecting her young? That made a peaceful solution that much less likely.

Predators were dangerous but could be frightened off. A mother protecting her children was much less likely to run to keep herself safe.

Carefully looking back, I saw Lisa edging around the cab of the rover and out of sight. Good. She'd be safe, or at least safer, and that was my main objective. Hopefully the humans would get the rover started and off the path — then once the animals were past, we'd move on.

But luck wasn't with us tonight. Perhaps following my gaze, perhaps just judging the rover as the bigger threat, the animal turned back to the vehicle. My blood ran cold and I shouted.

"Hey! Over here!" Waving my hands wildly, I jumped closer, hoping that would get its attention. Its head snapped back, horns lowered, and it roared another challenge. I drew a blade and roaring back, making myself as much of a threat as possible.

Angry eyes flickered between me and the rover. But as dangerous as I made myself look, the big white vehicle blocked the trail, and that made it the greater problem.

When the beast lowered its head and charged, it was like a mountain rushing forward. The ground shook as it rumbled forward faster than anything that size had any right to move. I swore and launched myself into its path, throwing a dagger at its eye.

For a moment I thought I might succeed, but no. The blade struck a boney protrusion next to the eye and skittered harmlessly off, vanishing into the night. Not even noticing my attack, the animal rushed for the rover, Lisa diving for cover amongst the trees.

I struck the animal's side, grabbing hold of its thick white fur with one hand, the other drawing a fresh blade and stabbing. The tip barely scratched the monster's skin, even the hardened hullmetal blade not enough to cut deep. I barely had time to curse before the charge struck the rover.

While my blade couldn't punch through the monster's hide, its horns had no trouble with the plastic hull of the human vehicle. The rover rocked back, tearing open, and I heard a scream from the cab. Malcolm hadn't left his post at the controls, a brave but foolish choice. I swore: keeping my khara's brother safe wouldn't be easy if he refused to do the sensible thing and *run away*.

Putting all my weight and strength behind it, I drove my knife down again. This time the point dug in a hand's width before getting stuck. Dark blood welled out of the wound and at last I had the animal's attention. It bucked under me, twisting and trying to dislodge me.

I howled a hunter's call and stabbed again, but there was no hope of reaching a vital organ. I could only hurt this monster, not kill it — but if I kept its attention off the humans and their vehicle, I'd take that.

A third stab wound was enough to convince it to scrape me off against the nearest tree, smashing its flank into the wood and sending up a cloud of glowing insects as I went flying. Long years of practice and training kicked in and I hit the ground in a roll, tumbling over and over before bouncing to my feet still holding a bloody blade.

A quick self-check: bruises, nothing more serious. I'd been lucky. I couldn't count on that happening again but staying out of the fight wasn't an option. Lisa was back there somewhere, and I would *not* leave her as prey for that monster.

The lights moved behind the undergrowth, Malcolm trying to turn the rover off the path. I burst out of the brush just in time to see the beast's horns tear into the rover's cabin, a scream of shock and pain echoing in the night. Fear and rage mixed in me and time seemed to slow.

No time for a clever plan or even a good one. I had to take a chance again, and this one would be suicide if it didn't work. But I didn't have a choice. This animal wasn't stopping, and we needed the rover desperately if we were going to get anywhere.

Screaming a challenge, I charged.

The beast saw me coming. Turned to face me, horns low, points gleaming. Instead of turning aside or trying to jump over them, I ducked under, dropping and letting my momentum carry me under that monstrous mouth. It snapped at me, missing by a finger breadth, and then I was beneath it, looking up at its underbelly.

My knife struck up almost without conscious choice on my part. If the monster had a moment to adjust, all it needed to do was stamp on me and I'd be dead. Everything hinged on my gamble that the creature's underbelly wasn't as tough as the rest of it.

Hullmetal blade met leathery hide, sliced through, bit into organs beneath. The animal roared, in pain rather than anger this time, and I cut with all my strength. Blood and guts rained down as I opened its stomach and the mighty creature spasmed above me.

And collapsed.

Dropping onto me.

My last thought before it struck was of Lisa. If I'd saved her, being crushed like this would be worth it. If not, then an ignominious death was all I deserved.

∽

I DON'T KNOW how long I lay trapped under the monster before the darkness moved above me. With a heave, I pushed at the vast weight lying on me and felt it give. Distant voices, muffled and unintelligible, called out as I struggled, and then the weight shifted. An engine roared and the corpse rolled away, uncovering me.

Suddenly I could breathe again. I sucked in air, tasting the sweetness of oxygen and laughing.

I hadn't expected to survive that. A quick check told

me I hadn't even suffered a major injury. Lots of bruises but no broken bones, no damage that wouldn't heal quickly. Lisa and Malcolm looked down at me, as amazed as I was. For a moment none of us moved, then I cautiously stood.

As I rose, Lisa hit me in a tackle-hug that nearly took me off my feet again.

"I thought you were *dead* under there," she sobbed, arms wrapped around me tight enough to squeeze the breath from me.

"Careful," I gasped, lifting her up and grinning. We both lived! There was still hope that this cursed planet might hold a future worth fighting for.

Her grip loosened a little, letting me get some air. We held each other and I looked around, counting the cost of that fight.

The rover, thank the ancestors, still functioned. Chains linked it to the corpse of the creature I'd slain, explaining how the humans moved that incredible weight. The creature's horns had torn the hull but nothing that would stop us driving on.

Good. We'd need it more than ever, because I wasn't the only one injured in the animal attack. Malcolm limped aside, his leg bleeding where the beast's horn caught him through the rover's hull.

"It's nothing," he said, catching my look and straightening up. "I can manage."

Of course he put a brave face on his injury — he had my mate's blood, it was no surprise he shared her courage — but I knew that he lied. The bloody wound needed medical attention, more than we had to offer here. The autodoc back at the colony pod would work. Hopefully the humans at our destination had one available.

"We need to get you to a medic as soon as possible," I said, Lisa nodding quickly. "In the meantime you should rest."

"I'm fine," he protested, only for Lisa to fix him with a glare.

"You're not," she said, voice shaking a touch. "But you will be, just as soon as we get you to the valley."

She hid her worries well, but not so well I couldn't see them. I put an arm around my khara's shoulders, comforting her.

"We will set off at once," I told her. "Don't worry. We'll make it, and your brother can rest his leg on the way. It will be fine."

It has to be fine. I had to take it on faith myself — humans were fragile compared to prytheen and had no healing trance to help put themselves back together. But there was nothing else I could do beyond support her.

She nodded, smiling unsteadily and pulling herself up into the driver's seat. I lifted Malcolm up beside her, pretending not to notice his wince of pain. No need to embarrass the boy.

While Lisa bandaged her brother's wound, I checked the rover's cargo space. A quick look showed that the stasis tubes were untouched by the violence. Green lights showed that all was well. Good.

Stepping out, I began to forge a path off the trail, leading the rover into the woods. That had always been the plan, though I'd hoped to follow the trail a while further before leaving it. That wasn't an option anymore, not when it took the risk of running into more of those shaggy monsters.

Our progress was slow now: not only were we pushing into completely unexplored terrain without even an animal path to guide us, but I had to make sure we didn't leave an easy to follow trail of our own. Gurral might have given up the chase but I didn't want to bet on it, and the last thing I wanted to do was leave him an easy path.

Malcolm and Lisa took turns driving and sleeping, Lisa shouldering most of the burden. But she couldn't stay awake forever, and Malcolm wanted to be useful. His injured leg didn't keep him from driving, and that let us keep moving with only short breaks.

I'd learned enough about Crashland to avoid the obvious dangers, skirting the territories of dangerous predators where I saw their signs. Again, that slowed us. But it made our path unpredictable, and a less skilled hunter trying to follow us might blunder into the lair of a hunting beast.

Despite the danger of our journey, I started to relax into it. Now I could use my skills as a scout to find us a safe route to our destination, it felt like this was what I'd been born for. If it hadn't been for Malcolm's injuries, I'd have even enjoyed the journey — but they gave us an urgency that stripped the joy from the trip.

I ranged further and further ahead seeking the fastest route for the rover, then ducking back to cover our trail. We moved slowly, but the hovering vehicle left few tracks and our hunters weren't skilled trackers. Once a day passed, I started to feel safe. Anyone behind us would surely have lost the trail.

Two more days passed before our path reached the top of a cliff. Below us a fast-running river rushed past on its way down from the mountains, and I grinned to see it. We were near our goal now — this river would lead us to the valley if we followed it.

All we had to do was follow the river until we met the border of the human settlement we were looking for. How they'd react to my arrival was an open question, but I was content to leave that for the future. As long as Lisa got there in one piece I'd be happy, whatever happened to me.

Snow-capped mountains rose on either side of our destination and I grinned, estimating the distance we had left to cover. In half a day, Lisa would be safe, Malcolm would see a doctor, and Maria, Alex, and Tania could be woken from their sleep.

Sundered space, we've really made it, I thought. And that was the moment that the rover's engine cut out, dropping it to the forest floor with a crunch.

19

LISA

I woke from a dream of flying with a scream as the rover dropped out from under me, Malcolm shouting a warning from the driver's seat. For a moment I didn't know where I was, everything was chaos, and I was falling.

Then I remembered.

We were on the run. Malcolm was taking his turn driving. And he'd *crashed our only hope of getting to safety.*

"What did you do?" I demanded, pulling myself up and scrambling for the controls. Red warning holograms floated in the air above the dashboard and the controls did nothing.

"I didn't do anything," Malcolm protested, yanking the start lever with unnecessary force. The engine stayed obstinately silent and the rover refused to rise from the ground. "It just stopped!"

I looked up, out of the window, and saw the drop

down to the fast-flowing river only a few inches away. My heart skipped a beat and I thanked my lucky stars we hadn't skidded over the edge into the white water below.

Torran bounded back out of the trees ahead, sliding to a stop and looking at us through the windshield. I waved to show we were okay, and he relaxed a touch. Not much though, and I couldn't blame him for that.

Without the rover we were stuck. The stasis tubes were far too heavy to carry out of here, and on our own we couldn't open them. Alex, Maria, and Tania were trapped until we got them to a facility with an autodoc.

I pushed the door open, looking at Torran, then at the mountains. They weren't that far away… maybe we could manage the rest of the journey on foot.

"How close are we to the valley?" I asked, carefully leaving the cab.

Torran cocked his head to the side, looked at the sky though the trees, then back at me. Shrugged. "A few of your hours at the speed we've been traveling. I could do it in half that, alone."

I sighed in relief. Close enough. "Okay. In that case we can trek in and get help if we can't get the rover started again."

Torran nodded reluctantly, looking at Malcolm. I winced. With his injured leg, he wouldn't be able to make much speed. Fine. Time for a new plan.

"You can get there fastest," I told Torran. "Hurry

there, hurry back. We'll wait here — we'll be safe in the rover."

The tears in its hull put a lie to my words, but it was still the best idea I could come up with. Torran disagreed, shaking his head emphatically.

"I will not abandon you here, my khara," he said. "The wildlife is too dangerous. Besides, it would not work. A human approaching the valley will be greeted with caution. A prytheen warrior? They'll shoot me as soon as I make myself known."

I put my hands on my hips, exasperated. He wasn't *wrong*, but that didn't make what he said any less frustrating.

"Okay then. I'll go, you two stay here."

"You will not." Torran's tone brooked no defiance. "The journey is too dangerous for you alone."

"There's no other way forward, Torran," I said, desperate for a solution. "Malcolm can't walk that far, even if we're willing to leave the rover behind with the others. We aren't leaving my brother here on his own."

Bad enough for both of us to wait here, but I would *not* abandon Malcolm. Especially not with an injured leg.

"I can carry him," Torran said. He didn't sound happy with that plan, and I didn't blame him. The forests of Crashland weren't safe, and he'd be our only defender on the journey. It would still mean abandoning Alex, Maria, and Tania. I chewed on my lip, trying to think of a better option.

"Hey," Malcolm called from the cab. I turned,

hoping the rover had come back to life, but no. The control lights were still all red, warning after warning. Malcolm wasn't looking at them, though. He'd brought up the communications display, the one we'd ignored since leaving the colony. With no one in range, there'd been no point — but unlike the controls, the comms lights glowed green.

"I've got a communicator contact," Malcolm said, talking quickly. "I thought maybe we were close enough to the valley to reach them and call for help."

It was a miracle. I grinned, a weight lifting from me. If we were close enough to one of the valley colonists to contact them, our problem was solved. They could send a rescue party and whatever was wrong with the rover wouldn't matter. Giddy with relief, I pulled myself back up next to my brother and reached to open a channel.

Paused.

Something was wrong. It wasn't an unknown signal.

I switched Henry on, looking at the contact on my own display to check. Henry barked and my jaw tightened.

"That's Carrington's comm," I said, staring at the display and blinking quickly. "How can we be picking that up this far from the colony?"

I knew the answer as soon as I asked the question. No way the comm's range stretched as far as we'd traveled — which meant he was close by. I spun to look at the forest, half expecting to see him striding out of the trees.

My mind raced. He was close enough to contact the rover, and that explained the sudden stop. Carrington had the authority to stop the vehicle remotely — I might be able to override that, but it would take time we didn't have. If he'd kept himself logged into the vehicle, he'd been able to follow our path, the safe route Torran had scouted.

He'd be close on our heels, but he wouldn't be alone. For all that he liked to think of himself as a ranger, Crashland's wildlife would have eaten him alive. If he was here, then so were the prytheen.

I didn't need to tell Torran. He worked it out as fast as I did, stepping between me and the forests, knife in hand and eyes searching for enemies.

"Run," he hissed. "Take your brother and go while I hold them off."

Torn, I stared at him. Abandoning him like this seemed impossible but if I stayed I'd just be damning myself and Malcolm to slavery or death. On the other hand, did we even stand a chance of making it to the valley on our own?

We had to try. If it had just been me, I'd have stayed and fought alongside Torran — however futile it was, better that than leaving him behind. Malcolm was my responsibility though, and I had to get him to safety.

"Come on," I said, pulling myself together and grabbing my brother's shoulder. I'd carry him if I had to. "We're getting out of here."

"No you are not." Gurral's cold, hard voice stopped me before Malcolm had clambered out of the rover. "As amusing as hunting you in the woods might be, I will not take the chance that you'd get away."

Half a dozen Prytheen warriors emerged from the woods, grinning at us. Behind Gurral followed Mr. Carrington, his ruddy face strained and sweat-stained. Keeping up with the hunters hadn't been easy for him and I wondered if the aliens had carried him part of the way.

More important than his company was the rifle Gurral carried. He rested it easily across his shoulder I knew it would take only a moment for him to get it ready to fire. Two of the other prytheen carried rifles too. I swallowed. Against these odds, fighting would be suicide.

The prytheen spread out, keeping their distance as they circled us. Gurral watched us with cruel interest, his eyes gleaming.

"Let them go," Torran said, shifting his weight from side to side as he tried to watch all the approaching enemies. "The humans are nothing to you."

"Oh no," Gurral said with a laugh. "No, they are *everything*. If they escape, they'll alert the other humans in the valley, and I can't have that. Not when you've been kind enough to lead me so close to my prize."

I gasped, glancing in the valley's direction. Yes, we'd cleared a path all the way here. Nearly to the gates of the unsuspecting settlement. It wouldn't have mattered if Gurral hadn't been able to follow us so closely —

another day and the colony would be warned and ready for an attack. But without warning? They were in deadly danger.

And that was down to one person.

"How could you?" I shouted at Carrington, ignoring the prytheen for a moment. Oh, they were slaving bastards — but he'd sold out his own kind. "You led them here, you shut down the rover. Why?"

He drew himself up to his full height, blustering and furious. "You don't get to judge me, girl. I made the rational choice, and if you weren't so blinded with lust for your alien lover, you'd see it too. Prytheen will conquer the valley — if it's not Gurral, it will be someone else. Living in denial is pointless. We're better off making our peace with the inevitable and getting in on the ground floor of the new order."

Gurral's lips pulled back in what someone more generous than me might have called a smile. He might not speak English well, but he knew enough to follow Carrington's words.

"You see, Torran?" he said in Galtrade, making sure we all understood. "This human is clever. He's loyal, and he and his family will be rewarded. You, on the other hand, are a mewling traitor and will die slowly in a ditch."

As soon as Gurral spoke, I knew how Torran would respond. But so did Gurral, swinging down his rifle even as Torran bounded forward.

The distance was too great. Torran would never reach his foe, not before taking a laser blast to the face.

I cried out, diving sideways, tackling my alien lover and knocking him to the ground.

Hot light burned above me, the laser missing me by inches. My cheek stung from the sudden heat and my eyes watered, but I'd managed to turn Torran's suicidal pounce into an undignified tumble. We rolled to a stop as Gurral's prytheen warriors leaped forward, one grabbing Malcolm, another covering us with his own stolen rifle.

Torran's arms folded around me and fresh tears well up in my eyes. This was *not* the embrace I'd longed for and it might well be our last one. I looked up at the weapons leveled at us and prepared to die.

"Stop!" Carrington's voice carried a familiar snap of command, sufficient to make even the prytheen freeze in their tracks. Gurral turned to his human follower, frowning, but the other two riflemen kept their guns on Torran and me.

"You promised that the humans would be unharmed," Carrington continued, a little less confident now that the alien warrior faced him. But to his credit he stood his ground, staring down Gurral. "That's the price I asked for my help and you agreed, sir. What lesson will we humans learn if you don't keep your promises to us?"

"None, if I kill you too," Gurral replied, swinging his rifle causally around to point it at Carrington's stomach. Around us other prytheen laughed nastily. Carrington paled, swallowed, shifted in place. The moment stretched uncomfortably and then Gurral lowered his weapon with a laugh of his own. "A small joke, human. Don't worry, I keep my bargains. I'm not a barbarian."

Carrington's answering laugh was nervous, weak. The relief on his face was clear and he pulled at his collar as he looked at me. I glared back, wondering if he expected gratitude from me. If so, he'd be disappointed.

"Get her out of the way," Gurral said, waving at a pair of prytheen warriors. Torran squeezed me tight, kissed my cheek.

"Do not fight them," he said, voice taut and full of the same pain that filled my heart. "Beloved, do as they say. Live. Remember me."

How could I ever forget you? I tried to speak but no words would come, the agony in my heart too much for me. I turned to meet his eyes, hoping he'd see how I felt. Words wouldn't have done it justice anyway.

He met my gaze, golden eyes full of pain and fear for me. Torran didn't fear his own death but the idea that I might do something to antagonize Gurral scared the life out of him.

Rough hands grabbed my arms, pulling me back and out of his embrace. I clung to Torran with all my strength, ignoring the bruising-strong grip of my captors to get a few more seconds of his touch.

Certain I'd never hold him again, I tried to commit every detail to memory. The rough softness of his skin, the strange and alien texture of it that somehow felt more natural than anything else I'd ever touched. The scent of him, subtle and powerful and manly. His strong and handsome face, a hard mask over the gentle soul that loved me as I loved him.

The way he made me feel, more than anything: the perfect match between our hearts that made me half-believe that fate really had put us together.

Except, how could fate be so cruel? How could it let us find each other only to rip me from his arms so soon after?

I tried to speak again, but all I managed to force out past the lump in my throat was a wail of loss and pain. Torran winced at that, mouthed some word I couldn't understand, and then the men holding me pulled me back hard and I stumbled away from my beloved.

The gunmen raised their weapons again, and I had to look away. This was more than I could bear to watch.

But Torran wasn't defenseless, not yet. As I turned, he moved, his arm snapping out with a glitter of metal. I gasped — he'd taken advantage of our embrace to palm a knife, and now he threw it in a hard, flat arc that ended in the throat of one rifleman.

The crack of laser fire filled the air, but Torran was already rolling aside and he took the remaining gunman by surprise. The shot only clipped Torran's arm as he bounced to his feet, charging with a roar.

Everything moved so slowly, as though we were trapped in honey. The gunman tried to adjust his aim, the rifle tracking Torran as he moved. Gurral had only just started to react, swinging his gun around. The prytheen holding me reached for their weapons and I threw myself back into them, tangling them up as best I could to buy Torran time to escape.

Escape wasn't on his mind. I should have known better. My mate's eyes were set on Gurral's throat and his hands held knives. His long steps ate the distance, and Gurral leaped back, teetering on the cliff edge, his first shot going wide. I gulped. Torran might make it. A spark of hope burned in my heart as I watched.

And then the laser hit him in the back. His charge faltered just a step from his foe, giving Gurral another chance to fire. The sharp crack echoed across the hillside, and Torran spasmed as it burned into him at point blank range. He staggered, teetering on the edge of the cliff, fighting for balance.

Torran's hand flicked out in a slash, long knife opening a fresh cut in Gurral's face and sending him leaping away to safety, but even I could see that wasn't a lethal wound. And then my beloved toppled forward, another laser blast snapping out at him as he fell into the river below.

I sobbed, covering my face with my hands. At least he'd gone out fighting, I told myself, but that didn't comfort me. Torran would prefer that to giving up; I just wanted him alive and at my side.

I scarcely felt the uncaring hands of my captors lift me and carry me away.

20

TORRAN

My body burned as I tumbled off the ledge, and I flung an arm out in a final desperate attack. Not enough. Gurral ducked back, the blade biting into his cheek but missing anything vital, and then I was over the edge.

Below me, water crashed over rocks. The world tumbled around me and it felt like I had forever to fall. My anger left me, the pain faded as I spun, even the sorrow I felt at losing Lisa loosened its hold on my heart.

There was no time for that now. I'd done everything I could for her — and I'd failed.

That bitter thought filled my mind and heart as I struck the crashing waves and they flung me against the rocks. Impact.

Then darkness.

21

LISA

Rough hands pulled me back against the rover, shoved me down beside Malcolm. His presence stopped me falling apart. It didn't make things better but with my brother there to look after I couldn't afford to fall apart.

Maybe he felt the same because he put his arm around my shoulders as though he could protect me from harm. The gesture helped a little, and I hugged him back.

We might die in the next minutes. No point in wasting them on grief, even if Torran's death tore at my heart.

"Where are the other escaped humans?" Someone barked the question at me twice before the words meant anything to me. Briefly I considered snapping back at the prytheen warrior, letting my pain out in a litany of insults and curses. But I had to live. That was what Torran would want, he'd tried to buy me time to escape, to survive.

I wasn't going to commit suicide by provoking this warrior. That didn't mean I had to help him though. I shook my head, gritting my teeth and biting back the curses I wanted to spit at him.

Anger flashed in the warrior's eyes and he repeated himself again, only for Carrington to interrupt him.

"The stasis tubes are in the rover," he said quickly, his badly accented Galtrade sounding desperate. "The other humans are locked in there until we reach…"

He trailed off, vocabulary exhausted, but he'd said enough to pull the prytheen's attention away from me and Malcolm. I breathed a sigh of relief, looking around at him. His red face was drenched with sweat and not just from the exertion of keeping up with his captors.

As the prytheen walked away, Carrington moved closer and crouched beside me. His eyes pleading, he spoke in English. "Don't antagonize them, Lisa. Just — just cooperate, do as they say, and you'll be fine. More than fine! We'll be in charge. You've seen the prytheen, their Silver Band can't organize anything. They need us."

I looked at him with all the contempt I could muster. "You sold us out, you got Torran killed and you'll get the people in the valley enslaved — so you can be the chief slave?"

Carrington's complexion reddened and he rocked

back as though I'd slapped him. I wished I had. My palm itched to hit him, but I restrained myself. I had Malcolm to think of.

My brother had thoughts of his own on the matter though, lunging at Carrington with a sudden burst of violence. Carrington toppled backward into the mud as I grabbed Malcolm and held him back. Around us prytheen laughed.

"They'll never respect you," I said. "You're a joke to them, you get that, right? The prytheen you're so keen to serve won't care when someone sticks a knife in your side one night. In fact whoever does it probably gets your job at the top of the heap. Maybe it'll be me."

A cold rage ran through me and I let it. Anything to fill the emptiness Torran had left, anything to distract from the howling void inside me now he was gone. Carrington tried to say something, met my gaze, and scrambled backward instead.

Getting to his feet, he glanced around and blushed brighter at the amusement of his prytheen allies.

"You're upset," he muttered, trying to salvage his dignity as he brushed himself off. "We'll talk more when you're feeling better."

I bared my teeth at him, wishing I had a prytheen's killing fangs. He seemed to get the message though, hurrying away.

"What are we going to do?" Malcolm asked when Carrington was out of earshot.

"I don't know," I said, deflating. My anger might feel

good, but I didn't dare turn it on the people who were really to blame. "For now we keep ourselves alive and look for a chance to get away again."

"Don't worry sis," my little brother said, trying to sound brave. "I'll look after you."

My eyes filled with tears and I hugged him tight. The sincerity in his voice was heartbreaking.

"Don't do anything stupid," I whispered fiercely. "We'll take care of each other, but if you get yourself hurt I will be *so* mad."

The whirlwind of my emotions buffeted me between fear and rage and I didn't know what else to say. Gripping each other in silence, we both shuddered and hid our tears. Each of us pretended not to notice the other's terror.

Henry whined and nuzzled up to me, doing his best to cheer me up. It didn't work, even he couldn't lift the veil of sadness that had settled over my world. Absently petting the holo-puppy, I tried to keep my mind off my pain but there wasn't much else to think about.

Eventually it occurred to me to wonder what we were waiting for. Gurral was in striking range of his target now, only hours away from the valley he wanted to conquer, but we were sitting still. The six prytheen kept a wary watch on the forest and I realized that there weren't enough of them for an attack. This must be the advance guard, those who'd traveled fastest.

It was faintly amusing to realize that Carrington had been forced to run ahead with them, but also impressive that he'd managed. I didn't like the man, but credit where it was due.

The sun dipped towards the mountains and the bright day faded into a cool evening. Around us the strange, beautiful but deadly sounds of Crashland's wildlife filled the air and the prytheen watched for trouble.

Out of the darkness, the rest of Gurral's troops arrived, dragging Carrington's family with them. The boys panted, out of breath after the long march, but the prytheen seemed fresh. Gurral gathered his troops, leaving two of them to watch us humans as they talked tactics.

I glared at the boys, then turned to look out over the cliff. It wasn't their fault that their father was a traitor, and I shouldn't blame them. At the same time, I'd never seen one of them challenge him and I remembered the way they'd acted before the prytheen arrived. No, I didn't have much sympathy for them.

They kept their distance anyway, talking with their father as the night's chill set in. The glances they shot our way weren't friendly, but I tried to ignore them. Above us Crashland's smaller moon shot across the sky, gleaming bright against the darkness.

I don't know how long it was before Gurral approached and gathered us humans to him.

"We continue on foot," he said, slow and careful as though he spoke to idiots. "You will stay at the back of our group, watched by Ervas and Dessus. And if any of you try to leave, make a noise, try to attract the attention of the humans we attack, you will *all* pay the price."

His gaze lingered on Malcolm and me when he said that, and the message was clear. The Carringtons looked at us too. If we tried anything, it wouldn't just be the prytheen that tried to stop us. Human traitors would too.

"Sir?" Mr. Carrington said, not content with waiting for us to make an escape attempt. "If we get much closer with the comms, they'll be able to reach the valley and warn them."

Gurral's grin widened as I glared at Carrington. I hadn't thought of that but it was true. If the humans in the valley wore their comms Henry would connect to their signals as soon as they were in range, and that would have let me send a warning ahead.

Not now that Carrington had spoken up though. The prytheen put an end to the idea quickly.

"Give us the wristbands," Gurral snapped. "All of them."

The Carringtons complied without objecting. Malcolm and I took a moment longer but there was no way to fight this. Henry vanished as I unfastened my wristband, and his absence was another loss I hadn't prepared for. It hurt a lot more than I'd expected.

Tarva gathered the wristbands up and tucked them into her belt. Perhaps it was my imagination, but I didn't think she looked happy about the situation. Whatever her feelings, though, she didn't argue with Gurral.

Carrington, on the other hand, looked almost smug as he clasped his hands behind his back. I regretted not hitting him when I'd had the chance.

Chin up, Lisa, you'll get another chance. It looks like we'll be locked up together for the rest of our lives.

I doubted that would be long, somehow.

Satisfied with our obedience, Gurral stood and turned away without another word, stalking off in the direction of the valley. The rest of his forces fell in behind him, following into the gathering darkness. They moved with a silent, deadly grace that reminded me they were all warriors, killers. Not as skilled as Torran, perhaps, but deadlier than any human colonist on the planet.

The settlement in the valley was doomed and there wasn't anything I could do about it.

Dessus gestured impatiently and we gathered ourselves and set off after the prytheen. They vanished into the gloom and had to hurry to keep them in sight.

"They're unstoppable," Carrington said, nervous glee in his words. His voice a whisper, he marched beside me and I wondered — if I pushed hard, could I send him over the cliff and into the river below?

Not worth the risk, I decided with some regret. He was bigger and heavier than me, it probably wouldn't work, and even if it did, the prytheen would probably throw me off after him. Torran wouldn't want that. He'd want me to live.

"They are not," I hissed back, limiting my response

to words. "Even if they take the valley they'll just run it into the ground like they did our farm."

"That's what they need us for," he said, trying to explain himself. "We can keep the place running for them, we'll be the real power, and they'll kill anyone who threatens us. It'll be hard at first, but you'll see Lisa — we'll end up running our own country."

I glanced at him. It wasn't easy to make out his face in the darkness but his desperation was plain to see. Carrington wasn't just trying to justify himself to me: he needed to convince himself that he was doing something worthwhile.

You're not going to have my help doing that, I thought, swallowing a bitter laugh. *If your conscience is eating you, good. You deserve it.*

"I bet that's what every quisling tells himself," I said. "And in the end, they all hang for it."

Not true, unfortunately. Plenty of collaborators profited from their actions, but it made me feel better to pretend that his doom was inevitable. And the barb did its main job of making Carrington shut up for a moment. The last thing I wanted was to hear his voice.

Dessus shoved me in the back, staggering me.

"Less talk, both of you," he growled.

That was fine by me. I stumbled into the darkness of the Crashland forest, following the nearest prytheen warrior and wondering how long it would take us to reach the valley. How long before the battle started and humans began to die.

Maybe, just maybe, if I found the right moment, I'd

be able to raise an alarm. I didn't know if that would make a difference, if they'd be able to defend themselves once they knew the danger they were in — but it was the only way I could think of to help.

It would mean my death, but what did that matter? At least I'd be together with Torran again.

22

TORRAN

The cold stones at my back were agony, the icy grip of the river pulled at me, and my muscles had no strength left. Heat and blood drained from me, my life ebbing away as I clung to a rock with all the grim strength I could muster.

But I would not die yet. Not now. Not when it would mean abandoning Lisa to her enemies.

Lisa. Just the thought of her name gave me strength and I pulled at the slippery rock, sharp edges cutting my palm like a knife. No matter. I couldn't, wouldn't, give up just because of a little pain.

But my fingers, slick with blood and water, slipped. The current tugged at me, almost took me, and I knew that if I let it carry me away, I'd never surface again. Crashland's fish would feast on me, and that would be that.

I saw my khara waiting for me, clear as dawn and twice as beautiful. Crouching by the river, hand outstretched, urging me on. I would not fail her. With a roar of effort, I flung out my good hand and caught hold of another rough rock. It dug into my palm, searing pain overwhelming me, but I didn't let it stop me.

Pain was nothing. Blood was nothing. All that mattered was getting to the shore. Getting to her.

Bright eyes watched me struggle, Lisa's mouth formed words I couldn't hear. I knew that she was just an image conjured by my blood-starved brain, a figment. Still she gave me the strength to carry on, to pull myself up onto the rocky shore and collapse in a panting heap.

"I'm coming Lisa," I said aloud, mumbling the words. My eyes fluttered shut, and it would have been so easy to give in to my tiredness. To sleep and rest, to fall into a healing trance.

It would have meant my death. Here, amongst the hungry animals of Crashland, with no help coming for me, I'd be dead long before my body repaired itself.

Fumbling at my side, I found the laser wound where Gurral had shot me. Braced myself. Pressed a finger into the hole.

PAIN.

I sat up with a jerk, biting down on the scream that tried to escape my throat. The call of sleep was banished, at least for now, and I took an inventory of my condition.

Two laser blast wounds. One in the side, one in the back. Both missed all vital organs, but that was the only good news. The wounds bled freely, weakening me, and if I lived long enough, infection would set in.

And they hurt as badly as anything I'd felt in my life.

Then there were the injuries from the fall. I'd hit rocks on my way down to the river and been smashed into more as the water carried me away. Not something to complain about; if the current hadn't taken me then Gurral and his men would certainly have finished me off.

But that left me covered in deep bruises and cuts. Maybe some minor broken bones. Every inch of me hurt and moving wasn't easy. I pulled myself to my feet gingerly, testing. Yes, I could support my weight. I could even walk.

That's something, I thought, looking up at the cliff that rose above the river with a resigned sigh. Whatever I did next, it would have to start with that climb.

Getting to the top of the cliff took too long and hurt too much, but eventually I dragged myself up. Panting for breath I struggled to resist the siren song of the healing trance, pushing myself to my feet and taking a deep breath.

Night had fallen during my struggle with the river, and alien stars gleamed overhead. Finding a route back to the rover would be the easy part of what I had to do now.

Once I caught up with Gurral, I'd have to fight. Swaying from foot to foot I wondered how I'd manage to face one prytheen warrior, let alone the number Gurral had at his disposal.

"No point worrying," I said aloud. "*How* doesn't matter when you have no choice. I *will* rescue my khara."

I saw Lisa's encouraging smile in my mind's eye and drew strength from it as I staggered towards my fate.

∽

By the time I reached the rover, Gurral's band was long gone. I bared my teeth in a silent growl, wondering how much further I'd have to make it before I found Lisa again. If they'd left already they must be on their way to attack the valley, which meant I had to hurry. Once they took the human settlement, they'd be much harder to attack.

Fortunately, they'd made no effort to hide their trail. And the humans were with them — their booted footprints were easy to spot. I breathed a sigh of relief to see Lisa's amongst them.

Following wouldn't be difficult, and even in my condition I would move faster than them. The problem was, what would I do when I caught up?

Maybe there was something I could do to improve my odds just a little. I made my way to the rover, pulling open the rear door and looking at the meager cargo we'd loaded. The stasis tubes waited, useless to me, but beside lay our scavenged food supply and, more important, Lisa's bag.

Thanking the fates that no one had taken it, I rooted through the stolen medical supplies. They were labeled in human script, but some of the containers I knew from Lisa's care in the colony pod sickbay. Spray-on bandages would close my wounds and came with their own disinfectant. I used up two cans of the stuff, hissing in pain as the icy spray stung my wounds. At least I wouldn't lose any more blood — until the next time I got shot.

The other medicines were harder to identify, and I had no time to experiment. I threw the bag over my shoulder, winced, and pressed on. Lisa might be able to make use of it once I rescued her.

I refused to think about what would happen if I failed. No point in considering that: in that case we'd both be dead and together in the afterlife.

The trail stayed clear, thank the ancestors, and I made good time following the enemy. They had to be cautious, watching for sensors that might alert the human settlement of their approach. I only had to make sure I didn't alert my prey, and that was a skill I'd drilled into myself until it was like breathing.

My steps made no sound, and soon I heard others disturbing the forest ahead of me. Humans and prytheen, moving together. I bared my teeth, creeping closer and listening.

Somewhere in the darkness a bird hooted, the sound startling the warriors ahead. A beam of moonlight illuminated Dessus's face as he looked around, almost straight at me.

I froze mid-step, counting on the dark and the foliage to camouflage me. For a heart-stopping moment he stared in my direction, frowning slightly. Then his gaze moved on, scanning the forest with commendable thoroughness.

He knew his job as rearguard, but this unfamiliar terrain made his task difficult and mine easier. I started to move again, step by slow step, moving closer and keeping the trees between us.

Beyond him I heard human footsteps and my heart pounded, so loud that I almost expected Dessus to notice. Lisa must be there, so close now. Almost close enough to touch.

No overconfidence. You're outnumbered, outgunned. Don't count this battle won before it even starts. As much as I tried to control my reaction, the fierce joy I felt wouldn't be denied. I'd found her again, and nothing would keep us apart.

I slipped around a tree, into reach of Dessus, waiting to hear him exhale. With no air in his lungs, he couldn't cry out when I struck without warning, aiming a punch at the base of his skull to knock him out.

He might not be a scout but there was nothing wrong with his reflexes. Something, some subtle hint, must have alerted him to my presence and he ducked at the last moment. Instead of hitting its target, my blow glanced off his head, knocking him aside, still conscious.

His hand came around in a wild slash that forced me back and he drew breath for a warning shout.

Desperate, I leaped on him, my weight forcing him down into the undergrowth, a hand over his mouth.

Dessus struggled in my grip, and someone called out his name in the dark. I winced, pinning him and slamming his head into the ground until he stopped moving. Taking a blade from his belt, I crept towards the other rearguard.

He called Dessus's name again, concern in his voice, and I cursed. As soon as he was sure Dessus was missing, he would raise the alarm. I had to silence him while I still had the chance. I moved quickly and quietly towards the voice.

"Starless Void, Dessus, where are you?" The other prytheen asked, and this time I recognized his voice. It was Ervas, Rarric's friend. Soon he'd stumble over Dessus's body. I took a deep breath as he drew close, steadied myself.

Ervas was no fool, and he'd drawn his own blade. Advancing cautiously, his eyes never stayed still, flicking across the forest looking for an enemy. But like Dessus he didn't have the skill he needed. Every prytheen warrior knew how to hunt, and most liked to claim that made them an expert.

But I was a scout. I'd trained for these moments of quiet violence for longer than some of Gurral's warriors had been alive. And no one would see me if I didn't want to be seen.

Ervas walked past, so close he could have reached out and touched me. The shadows hid me from view and his gaze slid away. As he moved on, I grabbed him from behind, sliding my stolen blade into his side.

His body spasmed and went limp and I lowered him to the ground. Listened for sounds of alarm. Nothing. The woods were quiet as before, slow footsteps breaking the silence as Gurral marched on.

Those two had been the only ones behind the humans, I realized as I paid attention. The rest were out front, their attention on the forest ahead. No one paying attention to my khara, no one stopping me reaching her.

I slipped forward, silently creeping among the humans, and found her easily. Eyes on the prytheen ahead of her, hand on her brother's shoulder, she made her way slowly through the forest.

My heart skipped a beat at the sight of her. Uninjured, as beautiful as ever, but carrying a grief that hurt to see. Her every step looked painful, and I knew how badly she mourned me. I'd have felt as bad if I thought her dead, and I wasn't sure I'd have the strength to carry on.

The temptation to grab her and her brother, to slip away into the night, was strong. I'd exhausted my energy reserves, and there were still far too many of Gurral's warriors ahead of me.

But I knew that was a false hope. Yes, we could vanish, but where would we go? With two humans in tow I wouldn't beat Gurral to the valley. And we had no supplies for a trek elsewhere.

Worse, I knew what Lisa would say. We'd led Gurral

to the edge of the valley's defenses, we had an obligation to stop him. My khara was fierce and noble and she would not want to abandon her kind to the mercy of a killer.

Nor did I. As much as I wanted to slip away, I knew we wouldn't be able to live with ourselves afterward.

As I moved forward I wished I could talk to Lisa, make sure she was alright. To show her I was alive. But the guard she followed was too close for me to risk it. He'd hear me if we spoke, and even if I just showed myself her reaction would give us away. Putting myself in Lisa's place, I doubted I'd have been able to keep quiet if I suddenly saw her again after being separated.

I didn't dare risk it. Instead, I slipped around her, near enough that I almost touched her. She never even looked up, eyes focused on the figure ahead.

I followed him too, moving just a touch faster than him. Just enough to catch up slowly, coming close enough to reach out…

At the last second, he heard me behind him and started to turn. My hand clamped over his mouth and my knife sliced across his throat before he made a sound. I ducked into the trees as he slumped to the ground, the harsh scent of blood filling the air.

Eventually Gurral would notice his troops were going missing, but until then I'd thin his numbers. When I finished, my khara would be free and her people safe. Either that or I'd die trying.

23

LISA

I'm not sure when I realized that I couldn't hear the guards. The change was subtle, but the prytheen following us weren't as quiet on their feet as Torran. The silence behind me made it clear that Ervas and Dessus had disappeared.

It wasn't easy to resist the urge to bolt for freedom, but I didn't dare alert the other prytheen. *Maybe if we just stop, let them carry on without us?*

That might work. The warriors would press on without us, unknowing, and Malcolm and I would slip away into the night. Only, then what? Surviving in these woods alone wouldn't be easy, and we had nowhere else to go. With a lot of luck we might be able to retrace our trail all the way back to the colony pod. More likely we'd be eaten by some monster in the woods.

Perhaps whatever had gotten rid of the prytheen rearguard that should be guarding us.

I chewed my lip, looking around into the darkness with more interest than I'd managed before. Carrington was a dim figure in the dark, and the prytheen I'd been following was...

Nowhere to be seen. I swallowed. If we were being stalked by some terrifying predator, at least it had started with our enemies. Heart pounding, I pulled Malcolm closer and forged ahead. I didn't have any better idea of what to do.

When I came across the body, I wasn't surprised. What did surprise me was that his throat had been neatly cut. A knife wound, clean and simple, not an animal attack. Feeling a little nauseous, I crouched and pulled a blade from the prytheen's belt and passed it to Malcolm, keeping one for myself. My brother kept his eyes off the body, shaking like a leaf.

Somewhere in the darkness, a voice cried out in sudden pain and fell silent.

A sudden flurry of activity followed in the dark as the prytheen realized they were being hunted. Gurral shouted something, a challenge or a demand, and the others answered.

A roll-call, I realized. And I grinned as I counted the replies. Fifteen voices called out. There should have been more than twenty. Whoever was out there had been busy.

My heart thumped with a sudden hope and I swallowed, trying to keep it in check. It couldn't be Torran. No matter how badly I wanted it to be him, no matter how much I longed for him to save me, it couldn't be him.

But part of me didn't believe that. That part of me was certain who was hunting the prytheen and didn't care what logic said.

It doesn't matter, I told myself, tugging on Malcolm's arm and pulling him back into the woods, away from Gurral's voice. No need to get involved in this fight, whoever or whatever might be attacking.

Lights came on in the dark, those prytheen who had flashlights illuminating the forest to try to catch their attacker. So much for the stealthy sneak attack, I thought with satisfaction. But one flicked in our direction, shining across me and Malcolm, and a prytheen advanced on us. The glare of his light blinded me, and I raised my hand to shield my eyes.

"Drop the knives," he shouted, raising one of the stolen rifles at us. *Does he think I did all this?* I almost laughed. The idea that I'd been able to kill all those prytheen would have been funny if it didn't look like it was about to get me killed.

Malcolm's knife clattered to the ground and I dropped mine too. The figure stepped towards us.

And then a figure stepped out of the shadows next to him, appearing as if by magic. A blade gleamed, red and wet, in the beam of light, before sliding in under our attacker's ribs.

With an awful, gurgling gasp, the rifleman dropped to the forest floor. His flashlight fell, tumbling, and for a moment I saw the man with the knife clearly.

Unmistakably.

Torran.

I gasped, heart soaring. It was him; I'd never mistake him for anyone else. Bedraggled, injured, bandaged and blood-stained, he'd come back for me.

Our eyes met, just for a moment, and I knew that I should never have doubted him. Of course he'd come back for me. Nothing would hold us apart for long. I couldn't believe I'd doubted my feelings, and all I wanted to do was run to him, embrace him, hold him in my arms.

Tend his wounds and make him better again.

Before I took a step, another laser shot cracked through the woods, burning light cutting through where Torran had stood. He twisted aside, rolling into cover as another shot burned into the tree next to him and lights shone in our direction.

I gawped, and the next shots would have cut me down if not for Malcolm. My little brother tackled me into the cover of a fallen tree as the prytheen blazed away blindly.

Malcolm whimpered, a strained noise. Looking at him, I saw panic and glee fighting for control and hugged him tight, trying to steady him. He might have saved my life, but now he panicked as the prytheen tore the forest apart looking for Torran.

Carefully, cautiously, I peeked over the tree trunk, looking around. No sign of Torran of course — if he didn't want to be seen, he wouldn't be. The prytheen turned this way and that, lights flashing wildly through the dark and trying to catch him. As I watched, a knife spun through one of the beams, hitting a gunman in the neck. The prytheen dropped like a stone, blood spraying.

I pushed Malcolm's head down, keeping him from watching. This wasn't anything for my little brother to see.

Gurral snapped a command in prytheen and his remaining troops fanned out in the direction the knife had come from. I swallowed. The odds against Torran were still long, and if someone got lucky that would be the end of this. Plus he was already badly hurt: facing Gurral in a head-on fight might go badly for him.

I knew Torran wouldn't let his wounds stop him from facing down every one of these bastards if he had to, even if it killed him. That would be too much for me to bear. I had to help, had to do something.

"Stay here," I whispered to Malcolm before creeping out of cover. I kept low to the ground, crawling in the dark towards the fallen prytheen's flashlight.

It wasn't the light that interested me, though. I wanted his rifle.

The weapon felt heavy in my hands as I lifted it, heavier than I remembered. I tried to shake off memories of the last time I'd used a rifle but it wasn't easy. Trying to distract myself, I checked the weapon. The trigger guard had been snapped off making room for the prytheen's larger finger and it didn't feel safe.

That was alright. I didn't want safe, I wanted something dangerous to my enemies. Pulling myself into cover, I looked around for a target in the darkness.

In the woods, someone shouted, a mix of pain and triumph. Metal clashed, and the prytheen rushed towards the sounds. My breath caught as I tried to remember my lessons. A shadow ran through my sights and I squeezed the trigger more by instinct than design.

The laser bolt tore into the prytheen warrior, sending him tumbling to the ground. I gulped and rolled back into cover, not wanting to stay in one place. Given how good the prytheen's senses were, that just seemed like an invitation for them to catch and kill me.

Not that I would be safe crawling through the brush, but if I kept moving at least I'd be a harder target.

Can we win this fight? I tried to keep that question pushed deep down out of my mind, but it wasn't easy. And the obvious answer was no. Just the two of us against far too many enemies, Torran was badly injured, and I had so little idea of how to fight. Eventually one of us would run out of luck unless we tried something different.

I took a deep breath, rolled into the hollow beside a tree, and tried to think. Killing Gurral and all of his men seemed like an impossible goal, but the prytheen wouldn't give up while they could still win.

So stop them winning. I blinked as an idea occurred to me. For Torran and me and Malcolm, this fight was everything. For Gurral, though, it was just a distraction from his actual goal. He wanted the valley, not us.

What if I can keep him from getting that?

That gave me a goal I might be able to do something about. Maybe. I'd still need to be lucky but at least I knew what I was doing. I just needed to find my target.

Fortunately, that was an easy task. He'd be the only prytheen with glowing lights attached to his belt.

My hands shook as I looked around the tree, raising the rifle slowly. I bit my lip, the pain helping me focus as I sucked down ragged breaths. Lights moved through the trees, prytheen shining their flashlights around wildly. There were less of them now — either Torran had been busy whittling down their numbers or some of them preferred to stumble in the dark rather than advertise their position.

Or both.

It wasn't easy to stay still and watch, keeping my breathing as steady as possible and waiting for a moment. I'd only have one chance at this, if that, and the longer it took the more likely that someone would spot me. Or worse, catch Torran.

There! I saw Arvid by the glow of the wristbands at his waist as he moved from cover to cover. I raised the rifle, took a deep breath and let it out. My hands steadied and a strange calm descended on me as I watched him through the scope. I focused on this moment harder than I had on anything in my life, the thump of my heartbeat deafening as I lined up the shot. All I could think of was the moment I'd first seen

Torran through my crosshairs. The moment all of this had started.

Something must have alerted Arvid. Perhaps he heard my breathing, Perhaps he somehow felt my attention. It didn't matter. His head whipped round, mouth open in a snarl, eyes wide as he looked into the darkness and saw me. A hand moved in a blur, knife spinning towards me as my finger squeezed the trigger.

The crack of the laser echoed in the woods, a blinding-bright line of light cutting through the darkness and into Arvid's chest. His blade hit the tree trunk an inch from my face, biting deep and quivering there as I gasped down a sharp breath. Tears welled in my eyes as I watched Arvid slump to the forest floor in a heap.

No time to panic, I told myself. This was the only chance I'd have, and I had to make the most of it. I pulled myself up, forward, fast but low. Somewhere in the darkness another shot rang out and I tensed. But it hadn't been aimed at me — or if it had, the shooter missed by a mile.

Praying it hadn't hit Torran instead, I skidded to a stop next to Arvid and fumbled at his belt. Pulled my wristband from the bundle and prayed that our march had brought us close enough to the valley for this to work.

Henry appeared as I clipped the wristband shut, looking up at me with his big puppy eyes. I glared a warning at him not to make any noise and whispered.

"Emergency call to anyone in range."

A bright red glow appeared around the wristband,

announcing the emergency. The other bands buzzed and let out a high-pitched warning sound and I backed away from Arvid quickly. I swore, wishing it wouldn't announce my location so clearly in the night, but there was no stopping that. An emergency was supposed to attract attention, and of course the other wristbands had picked up the call. I hoped that someone else would, too, before Gurral realized what was happening.

It only took seconds for someone to answer.

"Who's there? What's the nature of the emergency?" An unfamiliar voice. Somehow that took me by surprise. It had been far too long since I'd heard a new human voice and I wasn't prepared for the sense of relief it brought me.

"My name's Lisa, Lisa Hartman," I said, struggling to control my panic and keep my voice down. The last thing I wanted to do was attract the attention of one of Gurral's thugs — but getting this message out mattered more. "And if you're in the valley settlement, there's a force of prytheen heading for you. They're raiders they attacked my home and—"

"Slow down," the man on the other end said, alarmed. "We're under attack?"

"Yes," I hissed, struggling not to shout. "Or you will be soon. About two dozen prytheen, maybe less now. I'm stuck out here with them."

He swore passionately, then got control of himself. "We can find your signal. Keep broadcasting and we'll try to get you to safety and deal with those bastards."

There were other voices in the background, too faint to make out. But just knowing they were there was enough — I slumped, tension leaving my shoulders. I'd delivered the warning. The valley knew what was about to hit them and would prepare for the attack. They might even get here in time to help me, but that was secondary.

Whatever happened out here in the woods, they'd be able to protect themselves. Or, if not, they'd never stood a chance anyway. I'd done everything I could.

Now it was time to think about survival. About getting me and Malcolm and Torran to some kind of safety. And the only way I could think of to get all three of us out of here meant doing something even crazier.

24

TORRAN

The ring of hunters closed in around me and I tried to keep myself focused despite the pain. This attack had been a long shot and while I didn't regret my actions, it was clear I'd die here. That didn't matter — I'd bought Lisa time to escape along with the other humans. A chance to get around Gurral's men and on to the safety of the valley.

Except I had the sinking feeling she hadn't taken it. That she'd stayed to help me. A spark of rage lit my soul at the thought of what would happen if she got caught fighting Gurral's men, and I drew strength from that anger.

I needed every ounce of strength I could summon. The loss of blood was catching up with me, my limbs felt heavy, and the darkness at the corners of my vision wasn't just due to the night. How much fight did I have left?

Enough to take a few more of these sthec into the dark

with me. I braced myself, pushed off the tree and readied myself to pounce as an enemy came closer.

"Stop!"

Lisa's voice carried through the trees, loud and clear, and everyone froze in surprise. I turned toward her voice, seeing her stand up in the open holding a light that shone through the trees as she turned. *What in the Starless Void are you playing at? Are you trying to get yourself killed?*

The first to attack her would die, I promised myself. Gathering myself for a charge, I watched for whoever would make the first move — but our enemies seemed as confused as I was, and none stepped forward to take the challenge. Lisa kept talking.

"This is over," she said, loud and confident. I knew her well enough to hear the edge of fear in her voice, but I doubted anyone else did. "The valley knows you're coming, they're gathering their soldiers and they're on their way to hit you first. If you want to live, get the fuck out of here and let us go. You've lost."

Gurral answered from the darkness, angry and hate-filled. "Even if this is true, why should we not just kill you where you stand?"

"Because that gains you nothing," a new voice answered, crackling with static. A human female, speaking through the comm link. "We know where you are, we have more guns than you do and we're ready to use them. Our fliers are already on their way. Let your prisoners go and *get the fuck out of our territory.*"

I wanted to cheer her forceful voice. That was an

ultimatum that Gurral and his men would understand, and surely no one would want to die just for the chance to get their revenge on a single human? With a flier the humans could rain laser fire down on the prytheen from above. Our greater strength and speed would mean nothing.

Around me, the prytheen muttered amongst themselves and I felt the tide turning. They had no stomach for that kind of fight, no love for being the hunted rather than the hunters. Some slunk off without waiting for Gurral's decision, vanishing into the night.

I should have known better than to trust Gurral's reason, though. His rage was too strong to restrain with mere threats, and with his control of his clan slipping away he needed to do something to restore order. He roared and bounded through the undergrowth, grabbing Lisa with a contemptuous ease. She squirmed in his grip, struggling helplessly against his strength.

"This is not how it ends," he shouted. "I will not be robbed of my victory. Come out, Torran, come and face me or I will tear your khara limb from limb."

That should have woken an even greater rage in me, but somehow I found myself calm as I stepped out of the trees to face my enemy. Of course it would come down to this, the two of us against each other. It couldn't end any other way.

I would have been an easy target for any of the others now, my attention focused solely on Gurral. But none of them moved, watching me stride out to answer their leader. My eyes flicked to Lisa, checking for injuries. No, my khara was unhurt. Unhurt and outraged, struggling in Gurral's grip. I marched towards the two of them, baring my teeth at the man who'd brought so much pain to us both.

"Release her," I said, voice a low growl. "Release her and slink back to your stolen colony. You've lost this fight."

His eyes flashed, claws extending as he grabbed for Lisa's throat. And I lunged, crossing the distance between us in the blink of an eye, my fist slamming into his nose before I'd even thought about it.

All my training forgotten, I let the burning heat of my rage guide me. Gurral had hurt my khara, meant to kill her. Nothing could stop me punishing him.

Taken by surprise, Gurral dropped his human shield and lashed out at me with his claws extended. I ignored the wounds he opened in my chest. They were nothing compared to what I'd suffered already, nothing compared to the pain of seeing my khara suffer.

Instead of defending myself, I smashed my fist into his face again, all my weight and strength behind it. Pain blossomed in his eyes, pain followed by rage. As tough as Gurral was, he didn't want to face me alone.

"Kill him," he shouted, looking past me to his men. No one moved to obey, and I hit him again. This time he twisted away, ducked back, shielding himself from my punch. "What are you waiting for, fools? Tear him apart."

He blocked a punch, tried a counter. I knocked it

aside, snapped a jab into his face, felt his lip split. He howled in pain and staggered away.

"Not this time," Tarva said, speaking for the other prytheen. "You can't deal with this by yourself, then you don't deserve our help."

He yelled in rage, furious as he looked around. No one would step forward. No one would take his side. Their lights shone on us, illuminating the duel, and this was a challenge he'd have to face himself. His authority was slipping away, and he knew it as well as I did.

Snarling, he lowered his head and charged, hitting me in a tackle that carried us both into the muddy ground. Claws slashed at my neck and I twisted aside, driving a knee into his gut with all my strength. Gurral gasped, his grip weakening.

My vision swam, blood loss taking hold again. The weight of my injuries was too much to overcome and if Gurral kept me at bay I'd fall soon enough. I had to win the fight quickly, no matter the risks I took.

So instead of scrambling back and getting to my feet, I gripped him tight and clawed at him with all my strength. Flesh parted under my claws and Gurral howled with pain, giving as good as he got. Over and over we rolled, each trying to get the one blow that would finish the fight, neither having the strength to land it.

He's good, I thought, *too good. Even without my injuries, this would be a hard fight.* But I had one advantage over him. Something he couldn't match.

He fought for glory, for power, for *himself*. To win,

he had to survive. I fought for my khara, and that meant I didn't dare lose, no matter the cost.

Ignoring the pain, ignoring the fresh wounds and old ones, I roared and summoned the last of my energy. I forgot about defending myself, put everything into attack. My fist smashed through his guard as he clawed open the wounds on my torso. My blood flowed freely but I punched again.

And again.

Gurral's head rocked back, smashing into the ground as I poured on the pressure. He gave up on attacking, trying to fend off my punches. I didn't let him, snarling as I hit him over and over.

Desperation blossomed in my enemy's eyes. I didn't stop, didn't pause, punch after punch driving him into the muddy ground until he stopped resisting. Panting, swaying, I straightened up and looked down at him.

There was no fight left in him. He couldn't even raise a hand to block me, and blood splattered his face. I swayed, snarled, raised a bloody fist.

Brought it down in a final blow, driving Gurral's head back. His eyes went blank and he slumped, unconscious. I pulled myself to my feet and turned to face the others, all lights on me as I snarled at them.

Lisa's arm slipped around my waist, and I'd never felt anything so sweet as her touch. My mate was safe and so was I — no one else here wanted to take up Gurral's banner after his defeat.

After a long pause, Tarva spoke again. "It's done. You win. We'll withdraw."

I nodded, acknowledging her surrender. And acknowledging her leadership of what was left of this clan. The rest gathered around Tarva, looking from her to me to the unconscious form at my feet. No one wanted to challenge her.

"What about Gurral?" I asked. Tarva shrugged.

"His ambition brought us here," she said. "We had a good thing going in the forest before he arrived with his big ideas for expanding. He *fucked* us, and then he wanted us to get him out of the fight he picked. Let him rot here or slink off into the forest to live somewhere else, but he's not coming back to our camp."

I nodded, accepting her claim to the colony pod and the farm around it. They needed territory to retreat to, after all, or there was no reason for them not to fight to the death. And Lisa had already given up on that colony when we left it.

We had a new home to look forward to. I heard a flier's engines in the sky, getting closer.

25

LISA

The prytheen held their discussion in their own language, and I had no idea what they were saying. No, that wasn't true: I didn't understand the words, but the meaning was clear. We'd won. Torran had beaten Gurral, the rest of the prytheen accepted that. Nothing else mattered.

I hardly believed it, but we'd won.

As the prytheen held their council, the other humans emerged from the forest. Malcolm hurried to my side, eyes wide, and I hugged him tight. My brother was unhurt, thank god. The Carringtons followed, the four of them slowly stepping out into the light and looking at the carnage. They stayed well back until the prytheen finished speaking and turned away, walking back the way we'd come.

Once they'd left, the Carringtons dared come closer. None of them looked comfortable speaking to me and I had nothing to say to them. The silence stretched awkwardly until Mr. Carrington broke it.

"All's well that ends well," he said with cheer that couldn't have been more forced. He clapped his hands, faking delight. "Well done, Lisa, well done! Now we get a comfortable ride to the valley in a flier, eh?"

The sound of an approaching engine got louder as it circled, looking for a place to land. I looked up at the branches overhead, then back at Carrington's desperate face. My desire to punch him was almost overwhelming, but I resisted it. There'd been enough violence and I didn't need to add more.

"No." I looked into Carrington's eyes as I spoke. "You made your choice when you sold us out to Gurral. You're not welcome where we're going."

"That's not your decision," he blustered, mopping his ruddy brow with a handkerchief. "You aren't in charge of the valley."

"True, but how do you think they'll react when they find out what you've done? You didn't just sell us out, you tried to help the prytheen conquer them because you'd end up in charge. I don't think you'll be welcome there at all."

His jaw worked silently as he tried and failed to come up with a response. I could see him imagining possible reactions from the settlers, and none of them looked good. At best he'd end up hated and alone. At worst, executed as a traitor to humanity.

Not a risk he looked happy about taking.

"You don't have to tell them," he said, a wheedling

note entering his voice. Nausea filled me as he begged, lacking even the dignity to stand by his choice.

"You're right, I don't," I told him, watching hope shine in his eyes for a moment. Then I crushed it. "But I will. And so will Malcolm, and Alex and Maria and Tania when they wake up. You don't have a place with us, and I wouldn't risk our new home by inviting a snake like you into it."

"If you leave me out here, I'll die." His chin wobbled, and he sounded near tears. I winced, but this cowardice didn't make him any safer to be around. He'd been willing to see any number of people die for a chance at power, and he'd do it again if I gave him the chance.

"You can still crawl back to the prytheen," I said, keeping my voice firm. "They'll need workers for the farm, and you wanted to be in charge of the settlement. Now you get your wish."

His mouth opened and closed soundlessly, and I stared him down. This was the fate he'd wanted for others, let him work the fields himself.

"Go on," Malcolm put in. "If you don't hurry up, they'll get too far ahead for you to catch them."

Carrington looked from me to Malcolm, then up to Torran. No one who would listen to his pleas, no one who'd take his side. Deflating like a punctured balloon, he turned and hurried into the forest, following Tarva and her men on the long trek back to the colony. His sons looked at each other and then followed. I felt a little sorry for them but not enough to call them back.

They were adults, and they'd all willingly gone along with their father's plan. Let them deal with the consequences of their choices.

As they left our sight, I slumped back against Torran, feeling the strength go out of my legs. He caught me easily, lifted me and held me in his arms and let out a laugh that shook the surrounding forest.

"We won," I whispered, feeling the warm solid strength of him against my back. I could scarcely believe it. We'd won, we were safe, we were alive. An hour ago I'd been sure I'd never see Torran again, but now here he was with me.

"Yes, my love," he said, nuzzling my neck and sending a shiver through me. "Yes. We won."

Malcolm made a disgusted noise and turned away, and I blushed, pulling away from my beloved alien warrior with an embarrassed laugh. Yeah, maybe this wasn't the time and place to celebrate. Soon enough, when Torran's wounds were clean. And we had a bed. Yes.

The engine noise overhead grew louder, and the lights of the flier shone down, pinning us in a bright white glare. Torran shielded his eyes as I waved, and the craft lowered itself into the nearest clearing large enough to take it.

Taking my khara by his hand, I led him towards our ride.

~

IT TOOK a couple of tries to convince the pilot to let Torran aboard the flier, despite the presence of a dozen men with rifles and riot armor. It helped that Torran looked like he might collapse at any moment. Now that I got a good look at him, I winced at the sight — his body covered in wounds and spray-on bandages, I wondered if he would stay conscious for the journey to the valley.

But his broad, victorious grin wouldn't fade and he clung to my hand with such strength that I knew he'd be okay. And that he'd never let me go again.

I hope that's only figurative, I thought with a chuckle. *He's not going to get much hunting done if he's dragging me around with him.*

Not that I'd mind if Torran never left my sight again. The flier took a detour to pick up the Dietrichs from our abandoned rover before flying us back over the forest to the valley beyond. I stared out of the window at the place I hoped to call home. Farmland covered the hillsides, so much better than the cleared forest we'd been stuck with.

My heart pounded. In some ways this sight was scarier than the fight had been — what if they didn't let us stay? What if they didn't let *Torran* stay? I couldn't abandon him but taking Malcolm off to live in the wilderness wasn't an option.

They won't, I told myself, squeezing the strong blue hand of my alien love. He squeezed back, peering past me out of the window at the landscape, and I felt the tension in him. The worry that fate would tear us apart again.

But he faced the future with a stoic confidence I envied. Whatever the universe threw at us, he knew we could weather it. And it was hard to argue with that, after all we'd been through already. I leaned into his shoulder, drawing strength from him.

"If Gurral couldn't keep us apart, these humans won't either," he rumbled quietly into my ear. "No matter what happens, I will find a way to stay with you."

"*We* will find a way," I said back, looking at the lights pass by as the flier came in to land. "Together."

"Together," Torran said seriously. "Together, always."

The flier settled on a landing pad beside the central colony pod, one much larger than our own. More buildings spread around it, a town large enough to hold hundreds of people at least. Waiting for us were a dozen humans with rifles. Together with the squad in the flier this had to be most of the armed forces of the settlement.

It was almost flattering that they'd called them all together for just us. Flattering and intimidating.

Their rifles came up as Torran stepped out onto the landing pad, not quite aiming at us but close enough to make the threat clear. Torran moved with slow care, doing his best not to appear threatening, but I had to admit he didn't pull it off well. Even injured and on the edge of passing out he looked too dangerous.

I'd have been frightened too, in their place. Hell, I had been — I'd shot him on sight, after all.

"Welcome," a woman said, stepping past the armed guards and looking us over. I recognized her voice — this was the woman I'd spoken to over the comms. She had a look of caffeine-fueled energy to her as she looked us over, and I hoped we'd pass her inspection.

Apparently satisfied, she nodded. "Please come this way. You'll want to rest and clean up, I'm sure, but there are things we need to settle first."

One of the armed men put a hand on her shoulder and whispered something, but she shrugged him off with a glare that would have killed a lesser man. Waving for us to follow she walked off into the nearest building, leaving us to hurry after her. The guards exchanged looks and let us past, but I felt their eyes following us as we left the landing pad.

Inside was a large meeting room, a table made of local wood, walls decorated with freshly woven blankets. The difference between this place and our own rough attempts at a colony couldn't be clearer. The woman took a seat at the head of the table and gestured for us to join her. Torran's chair creaked under his weight as he sank into it gratefully.

"Welcome to the Vale," the woman said. "I'm Victoria Bern. Call me Vicky. I'm the Vale Settlement's elected Speaker, and I figure we need to get a few things sorted out before you can get the rest you obviously need. I'll be as quick as I can."

In person she sounded a little less intimidating than

she had over the comms, but the way she looked at Torran made me worry that our journey might not be over yet. I noticed that while she'd offered us seats, she hadn't offered food, drink, or medical attention. Nothing that made us her guests, nothing that implied we'd be here long.

If they wouldn't let Torran stay there was no question in my mind — I'd leave with him, go where he went. But what would that mean for Malcolm?

We didn't even know if there was another settlement in walking distance. And with Torran's injuries 'walking distance' might not be very far at all.

"Thank you for taking us in," I said, smiling as warmly as possible. "We'd, um, like to claim asylum."

Vicky laughed a little uneasily. "For you and your brother that's no problem. We welcome any human who's willing to do their part, and you've shown that you'll do that! For an alien warrior, though? His people are the reason we're stranded on this planet."

Torran leaned forward, then stopped as Vicky leaned back. Spreading his hands in a gesture of peace, he nodded.

"I understand that, and accept that my people have earned our bad reputation," he said earnestly. "I don't ask for your trust, not straight away. But I promise you — I am here as Lisa's khara, her mate. I wish to join your society, and I will obey your laws if you will let me. All I ask is a chance to prove myself."

"I'm not sure you understand how big a thing you're

asking of us," Vicky said. "Many of us won't accept you."

"I don't mind, as long as I can be with Lisa. And I can help. I know how prytheen scout, how we hunt, and I will teach your hunters."

"And without his help, Gurral and his men would have made their attack," I put in. "He's a good man and you can trust him."

"You're hardly unbiased," Vicky replied, but then she shook her head. "On the other hand, you have a point. He saved us a lot of fighting we couldn't afford, and I don't want to turn you away after all you've been through."

"You can't kick Torran out," Malcolm blurted, jumping out of his chair. "He saved us a lot. And if you kick him out, Lisa will go too and that's not fair. You can't do it, I won't let you."

Vicky looked taken aback by the outburst and I found myself caught between wanting to restrain my brother and cheer him on. It was Torran who spoke first.

"Do not be angry," he said, putting an arm around Malcolm's shoulders. "She is correct, we prytheen have given humans every reason to be wary. If they cannot let me in, then we shall find somewhere else. Do not worry, I will make sure you and your sister are safe."

Watching him comfort my brother, my heart swelled with love for Torran. And Vicky seemed touched by it too. She tapped her pen on the table thoughtfully, frowned.

Smiled at Malcolm. "How can I deny such a passionate appeal? Fine. I can't offer you a place here right away, but I *can* offer you a trial period. Six months and then we'll see where we stand. Don't make me regret that, okay? This is going to cost me a lot of capital at the Town Meeting."

I let out a breath I hadn't realized I'd been holding, reached across the table and took her hands. "Thank you! We won't let you down, you'll see."

"I hope not. I'm sticking my neck out for you, but we do owe you. If it wasn't for your help, we'd have been in a lot of trouble."

Malcolm almost bounced in his seat, eyes bright. "So he can stay? Really?"

"Really." Vicky smiled back at him. "At least for a while."

"Good," Torran said, finally letting his exhaustion show. The relief seemed to have robbed him of all his strength. "Now that's settled, I can pass out."

He slumped forward and I barely caught him before his head struck the table.

26

TORRAN

I drifted in the darkness of my healing trance again, but this time I felt safe. Secure. People moved around me speaking in a language I recognized but didn't know. Lisa's English, perhaps? Whatever it was, it flowed over me like a welcoming warm stream.

Eventually I rose from the depths of my trance. I kept my breathing steady, my eyes shut, listening. Instinct and training told me I wasn't alone in the room, and I waited to gather data before I stirred. Though I felt safe, my training insisted on being sure.

One person. A human. I took a deeper breath, caught her scent, and restrained a joyful smile.

Lisa. My khara. My one and only mate, right there in arm's reach.

So I did the obvious thing. Opening my eyes, I reached out for her and pulled her to me. Lisa shrieked at my touch, squirming as she fell onto the bed beside me.

"You *ass*," she said, outraged but giggling. "You could have given me a heart attack."

Immediately contrite, I let go of her. But she didn't pull away, instead snuggling up against me.

"I wanted to surprise you," I told her, kissing her neck.

"You did that alright," she said with a sigh. "You've been unconscious for nearly a week, Torran. And then suddenly you grab me? You're lucky I didn't punch you in the face."

She laughed, and I chuckled along with her. Looking around the room, I examined my surroundings. Prefab walls lined with blankets, colorful displays of fabric that kept in the warmth. Sunlight streamed in through a large window, and a hologram display on one wall showed a looping image of an ocean. Soothing, peaceful, and welcoming.

And definitely not a prison. The window was too big, the door too flimsy, for this room to hold me. I smiled, taking my khara in my arms and squeezing her against me.

"We're safe here, then? What has happened in this *week*?" It wasn't a time unit I knew, but from context I guessed it was long enough for things to have changed.

Lisa snuggled back against me, her firm body pressed to mine, immediately awakening my lust. My cock hardened at her touch and nearly forgot about my questions.

"Everything's fine," Lisa told me, wriggling again. Deliberately, I was certain. I growled a little and a delicious shiver ran through my khara's body. "Alex, Maria, and Tania are awake again. Lucky them, they slept through the whole escape. And Vicky's given us this room for the time being. We'll get our own place if they let us stay."

"*When* they let us stay," I corrected, pulling her closer and kissing her neck. "They have good reason to be cautious, but they will see we are a good addition to their community."

Lisa squirmed, breathing faster, and turned in my arms. Her flushed face was only inches from mine, and she bit her lip in a cute gesture I loved dearly.

I looked forward to finding out what other endearing faces I could get her to make. The experiment would take years — joyful, long, satisfying years.

Pulling her to me, I kissed her, gentle at first then more urgent. Lisa moaned and slid her hands around me, caressing me, peeling back the blankets that covered me. My body felt fully alive, responding to her touch and her presence.

And then someone knocked on the door. I growled, looking up from the kiss.

"Ignore it," Lisa said. "They'll go away."

The hammering grew louder, and Malcolm called out Lisa's name. She groaned and reluctantly pulled herself out of my grasp, standing and straightening her clothes.

"Of course," she said, shaking her head. "The day you wake up is the day he *has to* visit."

Frustrated and amused, I lay back on the bed and looked up at the ceiling. "The boy has amazing timing. It'll get him in trouble someday."

Lisa snorted an undignified laugh. "Someday? What's wrong with now? We can find somewhere to hide the body…"

I chuckled and shook my head, sitting up again and stretching. My body felt like a mess of pain, covered in new wounds, but all of it seemed to work. *Perhaps I should have checked that before pulling Lisa into my bed*, I thought, amused at myself. There was, after all, no urgency now.

My body disagreed. It wanted my khara and no delay was acceptable.

The door slid open and Malcolm's head peeked around it, grinning at me. "You're awake! Dr. Collins said you were."

"Oh? And how did this doctor know?" I couldn't help baring my teeth. Whoever had sent the kit to interrupt us had some explaining to do.

"Her clinic is monitoring your vital signs," Malcolm explained, entering the room. He carried a covered basket, and a delicious scent of cooked meat rose from it. "Keeping an eye on you from a distance. And she said you'd want something to eat."

My stomach rumbled and I grabbed the basket out of his hands. I should have realized how hungry I was

— several days in a healing trance had used every bit of fuel my body had.

"You're forgiven then," I said, tearing the cover off as Lisa watched with amusement. Inside there were packages of some kind of flatbread, wrapped around meat and vegetables. I tore into one without thinking about it. Delicious.

Lisa shook her head, and Malcolm frowned. "Forgiven? Did I do something wrong?"

I didn't answer, too busy eating, and Lisa replied for both of us. "No, silly, you're fine. And it looks like Torran really needed something to eat."

Starting on the second of the food packages I nodded, trying to slow down. Lisa carefully took the basket out of my hands and grinned. "Hey, if you're up to it, maybe we should take the rest outside and have a picnic? You've not seen the Vale yet, not really, and I'm sure you could use some fresh air."

I nodded, a little reluctantly. Right now every step away from the bed I wanted to share with Lisa was one too far, but if Malcolm was going to chaperone us anyway, we might as well. And I longed for the outside, for fresh air and sunlight. Unlike many prytheen I preferred the freedom of a planet's surface to the confines of a ship, or a room.

"Let me get dressed then, and you can show me our new home."

Our guest room turned out to be a chamber in the Meeting Hall at the center of the Vale settlement, and when we stepped outside we faced the colony pod that had brought most of these humans to Crashland. Far larger than the one Lisa and her companions had arrived in, capable of holding hundreds of humans in their stasis tubes, and all the supplies needed for the planet they'd expected to wake up on.

It was a testament to their species' adaptability that they'd been able to adjust to Crashland so quickly. This wasn't the world they'd aimed for or prepared for, but they were making it their home. I hugged Lisa as we walked through the still-growing settlement, prefab buildings arranged in a cluster beside the pod, farms stretching out over the valley. Woods beyond the fields, and an ultrasonic fence to keep out the wildlife. It would make a good home, I thought.

Settling down? Never thought I'd do that. Every planet I'd visited as a scout had been for a mission. There'd been an enemy to hunt or a target to find, and then I was off into the wild black of space again.

The idea that one of those worlds would become home had never occurred to me, not until now. Not until Lisa.

Humans watched us as we passed. Watched me, really, their eyes wary. I didn't mind — they had every right to be careful about a prytheen after we'd stranded them here. It might take time to prove I was a friend but whatever it took, I'd do it. Hard work didn't scare me. Only the thought of losing Lisa had that power now.

The settlement was still new, still growing, and it didn't take us long to get out into the untended areas. Purple-leaved trees rose towards the heavens, eerily silent. Ultrasound fences kept Crashland's wildlife at bay, and the species the humans introduced weren't spreading yet. I wondered what would happen when they did. What hybrid ecology would arise?

"Here," Malcolm said with a finality that amused Lisa and me. Somehow, he'd ended up in charge of our expedition.

He'd picked a good place for the picnic though, I admitted as I put down the basket and spread a blanket on the grass for us to sit on. We'd climbed high enough on a hill to look down at the settlement spreading in the valley below, the sun's light fell warm on us but the nearby trees offered shade if we wanted it.

I dug out another of the flatbread parcels and tore into it a little more slowly this time, savoring the subtle, exotic flavors of human food. The humans each took one for themselves, and we settled back to enjoy the view and the food in silence.

"This is delicious," I said when I'd finished. "I had no idea human cooking was so good."

"That's because Lisa's isn't. Remember the food she gave you when you were in sickbay?" Malcolm asked, laughing. Lisa laughed too, taking the jibe in good spirits.

"We didn't have much to work with back there," she

said. "Once we've got our own place, I can do a lot better."

"I will teach you prytheen cooking," I told her with a grin. "I've always enjoyed preparing food, but I've rarely had the facilities to do it right."

Lisa snuggled against me, looking down at the valley and smiling happily. "I'd like that. There's got to be some interesting fusion food we can make."

Malcolm looked at us, shaking his head again. "Sis, you never liked cooking."

"Maybe I just didn't have anyone I wanted to cook for," my khara said, sticking her tongue out at her brother, and we all laughed. The bright sun dipped low, heading for the horizon, and we basked in its rays.

But while the quiet moment was just what Lisa and I wanted, Malcolm started to fidget. I remembered being a kit that age, full of restless energy and always on the move, and I knew that I wouldn't have sat still as long as he had.

Even so, he didn't last long before getting up. "Sis, is it okay if I go and play? I think I see Tania down there."

I looked where he pointed. A small group of young humans were playing some kind of game with an oblong ball in a cleared area near the settlement and Malcolm vibrated with his eagerness to join in.

And I felt Lisa's eagerness to get him out of our way. An eagerness I shared — as much as we both cared for the kit, as much as we'd enjoyed our shared meal, we both wanted to get back to what he'd interrupted.

"Of course," Lisa said, making a credible effort at hiding her joy that he wanted to go. "Just be careful, okay? And don't stay out too late."

Malcolm gave her a *look* and grinned. "I won't!"

With that he was off, racing down the hill towards the other kits. We watched him go, sharing a smile.

"Now, where were we?" Lisa asked once he was safely away. I growled, my passion rising again, and stroked a hand down her arm. My claws extended, grazing her skin, and she shivered, mouth opening in a silent *oh*.

"You know full well," I told her, pulling her close. "And this time I do not mean to be stopped."

Her hand trembled as she tugged at my tunic, undoing its fastenings and stroking the skin beneath. I shuddered at her touch, growled hungrily, kissed her passionately.

Lisa's heart beat hard enough, loud enough, that its rhythm caught me and pulled me along. I pulled at her top, trying to be careful, trying not to damage it this time, but my patience had hit its limit. Fabric tore and she gasped, face flushing.

She pulled away, slipping from my grip and backing off as I followed. A bright, happy grin lit her face as she scrambled to her feet, and I advanced on her.

I moved forward. She stepped back, keeping her distance, maddeningly close but just out of reach. Her grin lit up the world for me, and I felt an answering smile spread across my face.

Lisa took another step back, towards the woods,

and I followed. My eyes tracked her, looking up and down her wonderful, beautiful body. Seeing the little shiver of anticipation I sent through her. Her need, her lust, matched my own.

She stared as I pulled off my tunic, her gaze roaming across my torso. Biting her lip, breathing faster, Lisa took one more step back. And then, with a laugh, she turned and ran into the woods.

I laughed too, bounding after her. The hunt was on.

27

LISA

Torran followed close behind me as I ran, and I knew that he could have caught me before I'd gone two steps. But neither of us wanted the chase to be over so soon. Strange alien trees closed around me as I sprinted, and he gained easily.

Never had a hunter tracked prey so eager to be caught.

I darted around a tree, trying to put it between us. Just because I wanted him to catch me didn't mean I was going to make it easy. And Torran didn't need my help. Looking back, I saw him pull himself around the tree, duck under a low branch, gather himself.

And pounce.

I tried to dodge. No chance. Torran was on me before I could move, his hands scooping me off my feet and carrying me to the ground in a tumbled tangle of limbs. When we came to rest, he had me pinned. Both of us panted for breath. I squirmed, testing his grip, and found myself unable to move.

I grinned up at my captor, my body trembling and ready for him.

"Now you've caught me, mighty hunter," I said, my voice husky. "What are you going to do with me?"

"Everything," he said, voice a low hungry growl that made me shiver with need. A strong hand pulled at my top, and all caution forgotten he tore it open with casual strength that made me gasp. Lowering his head, he kissed my neck, my shoulder. Trailed down to my breasts as he pulled my torn top wide, baring them.

A low moan escaped my lips as he licked and kissed and gently bit me. I squirmed, pressed myself up against him, my eyes squeezing shut. Torran's growl vibrated through me, a wonderful sensation. He needed me, wanted me, hungered for me as much as I did for him.

His kisses moved lower, down across my stomach, and his fingers traced patterns on my skin. Wicked, sharp claws brushed me with a carefully delicate touch, tantalizing and wonderful. I tried to reach for him, to touch and caress that wonderfully sexy body of his, but no. With one hand he pinned my wrists, with the other he tugged at my pants.

I sucked in a breath, looking down at him, seeing him grinning back at me. He was going to do this on his terms, and I had no problem with that at all.

A razor-sharp claw sliced the waistband of my pants open and Torran pulled, tearing them. Baring me. A few sharp tugs and he ripped them off in tatters. My panties parted just as easily, leaving me naked.

Helpless.

More aroused than I'd ever imagined possible.

"You are mine," he told me, lowering his head to kiss and lick and bite. His lips moved closer, ever closer to my pussy, and I could hardly bear the anticipation.

"Yes," I agreed eagerly. "All yours, always yours."

His hand released mine, brushing down me. Kissing my inner thighs, he parted my legs, cupping my ass in his hands and lifting me. I moaned, grabbing his head, trying to guide him to me.

Not yet. Torran enjoyed teasing me too much to make it easy for me. I shivered as his sharp teeth gently nipped the sensitive skin between my legs, oh so close to what I wanted. What I needed. Edging closer, but not giving me what I longed for.

"Please, Torran," I begged, panting. "Oh god, please? I need you."

Relenting, he brought his mouth to my pussy, tongue darting out to taste me, and I cried out in delight. My body arched, my fingers tightened in his hair, and his tongue danced across me expertly. Parting my folds, driving me wild, teasing my clit as I shuddered and writhed under him.

His fingers tightened on me, lifting me to him as he lapped at me. My mind went blank, all thought drowned out by the flood of pleasure he sent through my body. Gasping, shuddering, clinging to him, I lost all control as his tongue played my body like an instrument.

With a howl of joy I came, shuddering and shaking, Torran's touch too much to bear any longer. The world vanished in a white-hot moment of pure joy.

My eyes opened to see Torran looking down at me, a pleased smile on his rugged face. I smiled back shakily, not trusting my voice yet. My fingers trailed through his hair, down along his shoulder, along his arm. Powerful muscles rippled under alien skin, and I savored every sensation.

Mine, I thought, almost crying with happiness at the thought. Against all the odds this magnificent man was my mate, my partner, and we had all our lives to explore and enjoy each other. And I intended to do a lot of that.

His eyes sparkled and he nodded as though he'd read my mind. A blush spread across my cheeks and I laughed at myself. *Now* I felt embarrassed? That wouldn't do. Sliding an arm between us, I reached for his belt.

I could have told myself that I was repaying him for the pleasure he'd given me, and that wasn't exactly untrue. It didn't paint the whole picture, though: I wanted more of him, wanted him inside me, filling me.

His hard cock buzzed as my hand closed on it, stroking gently, and my cheeks heated. Breath quickened. Torran's smile widened and he tugged at his pants, pulling them off quickly and casting them aside.

I groaned and bit my lip as I felt him swell, iron-hard, in my hand.

"Khara," he whispered, a low husky sound that made me shiver with need. "You are magnificent. Wonderful. Beautiful."

I swallowed, guiding him between my legs. Feeling him press against me, hard and ready and eager. His cock vibrated powerfully, making me shiver in response. How did he drive me this wild with just a touch?

Our eyes locked, and I felt his arousal like a physical pressure. It was as strong as my own, as wild and hungry, like my own soul's desire reflected in his golden gaze. For a moment we paused, motionless, savoring this moment of quiet.

Then he thrust, his powerful cock driving deep into me, filling me, making me arch and cry out again. Torran roared in triumph above me, driving me into the forest floor before pulling back and thrusting again. I clung to him, fingers digging into his firm flesh, urging him on wordlessly as his muscular body drove into me again and again, wild and hungry and eager. His lips closed on my neck, teeth digging in as his cock vibrated inside me, pushing me towards another orgasm.

Each moment pushed me closer, drove me wilder, and he knew it. Reveled in it. I felt his pleasure nearly as well as my own as my body gripped him tight. Locked together it was almost as though we'd become one person, one body. We moved in instinctive harmony, and when my climax approached again, I knew he was as close as I was.

My fingers dug into his skin, scratching like a wild animal, and he howled in joyful hunger. Thrust faster, *faster*, making me cry out.

When it hit, the orgasm struck like a freight train. I cried out, squeezing Torran inside me, my body shaking as wave after wave of pleasure rocked me. There was, for a glorious moment, no world outside the two of us. Our intertwined bodies, our pleasure, our love. I lost sight of everything but Torran, the glorious marvelous wonder of his touch.

The taste of him. The sound of his raw breath. The shuddering pleasure as he came, filling me, our bodies arching in unison. Crying out in joined passion, we held each other, letting waves of pleasure pound us until we washed up in each other's arms.

∽

I DON'T KNOW how long we lay there in the gathering night, wordlessly holding each other. Speech seemed unnecessary; we both knew what we felt.

My fingers traced over the wounds on Torran's torso, feeling the scars his fight to save me had left him with. Some deep, some shallow, some that would fade, some that would be a permanent reminder. A sign of what he'd gone through for me, for us.

Leaning over him, I kissed his chest, and he held me tight. The warmth of his body shielded me from the chill of the night air, but it was getting colder and we couldn't stay here forever. Eventually, I sat up and sighed.

"We should go back," I said reluctantly, not wanting to break the spell. Torran nodded, taking my hand and bringing it to his lips.

"I suppose we must," he said. "Though I would gladly spend the night in your arms under the stars."

"You'd wake up cuddling an icicle," I said, laughing and looking around for my clothes. Torran had done a thorough job of shredding them.

He chuckled. "I could build a fire to keep you warm."

"Or we could go find a bed under a roof, with a heater and blankets," I suggested. Torran cocked his head to the side, considering, and grinned.

"I suppose there's a certain logic to that position," he admitted, bouncing to his feet. I envied his casual strength. Even after all he'd been through, after a week in a trance, he still moved with an easy grace and power that no human could match. I abandoned my futile search for my clothes to watch him dress, admiring the way his muscles moved. It was a shame to see him cover that body.

Unfortunately, he wasn't going to get the same show. All that remained of my clothes were torn scraps, nothing salvageable after Torran impatiently undressed me with his claws. I sighed, looking at what was left. It wasn't as though I'd had any attachment to the outfit, but I didn't have many others.

"I'm going to have to teach you how to undo a zipper," I told Torran, mock-glaring at him. "You can't just tear my clothes off every time you want me naked."

"True. I doubt the local industry would keep up with us," he grinned at me, looking at my naked body in the starlight, and I laughed happily as I blushed. He fetched me the blanket we'd picnicked on and I wrapped it around myself. That would have to do for the walk through town — I just hoped that most people would be in their beds by the time we got there.

I took Torran's hand and together we started our walk down the hill to our home.

EPILOGUE

The house was finally finished. It had taken us six months to build it — not because it took that long to put together a building but because there were too many other tasks that took priority. Torran teaching the humans his hunting tricks, the colonists making sure we all had enough food for the winter that would be on us soon, everyone taking their turn on guard duty against the occasional prytheen raiders.

I'd been working the farms, getting my hands dirty with the other colonists, and I found I loved it. But I didn't like being a guest in someone else's home, no matter how gracious our hosts were. The sidelong looks Torran got were the worst of it, but it also felt like an imposition on the settlement. Now we'd have our own space and we could do what we liked with it.

Torran looked down at me and I blushed, knowing exactly what we both wanted to do first. Having more privacy would be good for a lot of reasons, but there was one that neither of us could keep our minds away from.

Six months hadn't done a thing to dampen the flames of our desire. I doubted anything would.

"So this is where you'll be hiding," Maria said, breaking into our thoughts with a knowing grin. I coughed and looked away, leaving it to Torran to answer.

"Yes, this will be our home," he said. "But we will not hide here. You and Alex will always be welcome as guests."

Another nice thing about having our own home — we could have visitors over without imposing on our hosts. I looked forward to that, to being a proper part of the community that had adopted us. Over the past months Torran's hard work had overcome most people's animosity to the prytheen and we'd been cautiously welcomed into the family of the Vale. Now we had a chance to repay people for their patience and their friendship, and that felt good.

Well. Not *now*. In a few days, once we'd settled in and made the place our own. Then we'd have a big party.

Maria coughed and I realized I'd gotten sucked into my thoughts again. "Sorry, I've got a lot on my mind."

"I bet," she said with a grin. "I won't keep you, I just wanted to see the place now it's finished."

Along with a lot of others, she'd helped build it. That was one of the many things I loved about my new home: the Vale was a community where everyone pulled together to *help*.

Life here wouldn't always be easy. We still faced plenty of dangers — the Vale was too far from the *Wandering Star* for protection, so we had to look after ourselves. Despite the ultrasonic fence, the wildlife was dangerous, and too many of the prytheen hadn't made peace with their human neighbors. We'd already had to fight off raids from some trying to take food or slaves or both. Torran fighting to defend the Vale had helped cement his position with our new friends.

But the community was strong, and we would weather that storm. It was starting to feel as though we could weather anything Crashland threw at us.

The view from the window looked out over the forests where Torran hunted. On the other side of the house we looked down on the valley, on the community we were joining slowly but surely, the farms where I'd work. I grinned happily at the thought. This might not be the planet I'd set out to colonize, but Crashland had something Arcadia never would have.

Torran. The love of my life.

That made it a home like nowhere else.

The End

Thank you for reading *Torran!* Please take a moment to leave an opinion about the book, I appreciate every review.

The next book in the *Crashland Colony Romances* will be out soon. If you'd like to hear more about my upcoming releases, and get a free novella, sign up for my mailing list:

http://my.leslie-chase.com/booksignup

ABOUT LESLIE CHASE

LESLIE CHASE

I love writing, and especially enjoy writing sexy science fiction and paranormal romances. It lets my imagination run free and my ideas come to life! When I'm not writing, I'm busy thinking about what to write next or researching it – yes, damn it, looking at castles and swords and spaceships counts as research.

If you enjoy my books, please let me know with a review. Reviews are really important and I appreciate every one. If you'd like to be kept up to date on my new releases, you can sign up for my email newsletter through my website. Every subscriber gets a free science fiction romance ebook!

www.leslie-chase.com

facebook.com/lesliechaseauthor
twitter.com/lchasewrites
bookbub.com/authors/leslie-chase

SCI FI ROMANCE BY LESLIE CHASE

DRAGONS OF MARS

The remains of the Dragon Empire have slumbered on Mars for a thousand years, but now the ancient shifters are awake, alive, and searching for their mates!

Each book can be read on its own, but you'll get the best effect if you read them in order.

- **Dragon Prince's Mate**
- **Dragon Pirate's Prize**
- **Dragon Guardian's Match**
- **Dragon Lord's Hope**
- **Dragon Warrior's Heart**

WORLDWALKER BARBARIANS

Teleported from Earth to a far-off planet, found by blue skinned wolf-shifter aliens, and claimed as mates. Is this disaster or delight for the feisty human females?

1: Zovak

2: Davor

SILENT EMPIRE BOOKS

Romance in a Galactic Empire

Each of these books follows the story of a different woman, snatched from Earth and thrust into the Silent Empire — a galaxy-spanning nation of intrigue and romance. Read to see them find their alien mates amongst the stars.

Each of these books can be read as a standalone, though they share some characters.

- **STOLEN FOR THE ALIEN PRINCE**
- **STOLEN BY THE ALIEN RAIDER**
- **STOLEN BY THE ALIEN GLADIATOR**

THE ALIEN EXPLORER'S LOVE

Can Two Beings from Different Worlds Find Common Ground — And Love?

Jaranak is an alien explorer on a rescue mission to Earth, but now he's stranded here at the dawn of the 20th century. And his efforts to go unnoticed are bring thwarted by Lilly, a human female who won't stop asking questions. She should be insufferable, but instead he finds himself unable to get the sassy woman out of his mind…

MATED TO THE ALIEN LORD

a Celestial Mates novel by Leslie Chase

Love is never easy. Love on an alien world is downright dangerous!

With her life on Earth going nowhere, Gemma needs a fresh start. Enter the Celestial Mates Agency, who say they can match her with the perfect alien. And despite the dangers of his planet, Corvax is everything she could have asked for — impossibly hot, brave, and huge.

Now that she's seen him, there's no way she's going back.

PARANORMAL ROMANCE BY LESLIE CHASE

ARCANE AFFAIRS AGENCY

A shared world of shifters, vampires, far, and witches - full of everything that goes bump in the night! Check out the full list of books **here**.

THE BEAR AND THE HEIR, by Leslie Chase

When Cole North arrives in Argent Falls to investigate reports of magical storms, he doesn't expect much to come of it. Not after the series of pointless missions the Arcane Affairs Agency has sent him on recently. This time, though, it's different. The small town is plagued by bizarre weather, the storms are trying to warn him off, and there are *fae* running wild. And then there's Fiona.

No matter how much the bear shifter tries to focus on his mission, he can't get the hot, curvy girl out of his head. But the fae are after her too – and when they try and kidnap her, Cole's mission and his feelings for Fiona collide.

∽

GUARDIAN BEARS

Ex-military bear shifters providing protection from the threats no one else can deal with. Each book is a stand-alone plot, as the sexy bears find their curvy mates.

1. **GUARDIAN BEARS: MARCUS**
2. **GUARDIAN BEARS: LUCAS**
3. **GUARDIAN BEARS: KARL**

∽

TIGER'S SWORD

A four-part paranormal romance serial about Maxwell Walters, billionaire tiger shifter, and his curvy mate Lenore.

Box Set, collecting all four parts

1. **Tiger's Hunt**
2. **Tiger's Den**
3. **Tiger's Claws**
4. **Tiger's Heart**

Printed in Great Britain
by Amazon